Welcome to the Secret World of Alex Mack!

Just like everyone else I know, I've grown up believing in the truth. Honesty is the best policy, right? Wrong! Just try telling your mom her new casserole tastes gross. Or one of your best friends that her outfit makes her look like a bumblebee. Even teachers can't stand to hear the complete truth. I don't know what is making me tell people everything—I just can't stop! And that can be dangerous if you have a secret as big as mine. Let me explain . . .

I'm Alex Mack. I was just another average kid until my first day of junior high.

One minute I'm walking home from school—the next there's a *crash!* A truck from the Paradise Valley Chemical plant overturns in front of me and I'm drenched in some weird chemical.

And since then—well, nothing's been the same. I can move objects with my mind, shoot electrical charges through my fingertips, and morph into a liquid shape . . . which is handy when I get in a tight spot!

My best friend, Ray, thinks it's cool—and my sister, Annie, thinks I'm a science project.

They're the only two people who know about my new powers. I can't let anyone else find out—not even my parents—because I know the chemical plant wants to find me and turn me into some experiment.

But you know something? I guess I'm not so average anymore!

The Secret World of Alex Mack™

Alex, You're Glowing!
Bet You Can't!
Bad News Babysitting!
Witch Hunt!
Mistaken Identity!
Cleanup Catastrophe!
Take a Hike!
Go for the Gold!
Poison in Paradise!
Zappy Holidays! (Super Edition)
Junkyard Jitters!
Frozen Stiff!
I Spy!
High Flyer!
Milady Alex!
Father-Daughter Disaster!
Bonjour, Alex!
Close Encounters!
Hocus Pocus!
Halloween Invaders!
Truth Trap!

Available from MINSTREL Books

For orders other than by individual consumers, Pocket Books grants a discount on the purchase of **10 or more** copies of single titles for special markets or premium use. For further details, please write to the Vice-President of Special Markets, Pocket Books, 1633 Broadway, New York, NY 10019-6785, 8th Floor.

For information on how individual consumers can place orders, please write to Mail Order Department, Simon & Schuster Inc., 200 Old Tappan Road, Old Tappan, NJ 07675.

NICKELODEON®

the secret world of

ALEX MACK™

Truth Trap!

Cathy East Dubowski

A MINSTREL® BOOK

Published by POCKET BOOKS
New York   London   Toronto   Sydney   Tokyo   Singapore

The sale of this book without its cover is unauthorized. If you purchased this book without a cover, you should be aware that it was reported to the publisher as "unsold and destroyed." Neither the author nor the publisher has received payment for the sale of this "stripped book."

This book is a work of fiction. Names, characters, places and incidents are products of the author's imagination or are used fictitiously. Any resemblance to actual events or locales or persons, living or dead, is entirely coincidental.

A MINSTREL PAPERBACK *Original*

 A Minstrel Book published by
POCKET BOOKS, a division of Simon & Schuster Inc.
1230 Avenue of the Americas, New York, NY 10020

Copyright © 1997 by Viacom International Inc., and RHI Entertainment, Inc. All rights reserved. Based on the Nickelodeon series entitled "The Secret World of Alex Mack."

All rights reserved, including the right to reproduce this book or portions thereof in any form whatsoever. For information address Pocket Books, 1230 Avenue of the Americas, New York, NY 10020

ISBN: 0-671-01157-X

First Minstrel Books printing November 1997

10 9 8 7 6 5 4 3 2 1

NICKELODEON, The Secret World of Alex Mack and all related titles, logos and characters are trademarks of Viacom International Inc.

A MINSTREL BOOK and colophon are registered trademarks of Simon & Schuster Inc.

Cover photos by Thomas Queally and Danny Feld

Printed in the U.S.A.

To Christel Ann East,
a super sister and an awesome aunt!

Truth Trap!

CHAPTER 1

Alex Mack tried not to gag.

Her nose burned and her eyes watered as she tried to smile at her friend, Robyn Russo.

"Well?" Robyn asked, her blue eyes anxious above a face full of freckles. "What do you think? Be honest!"

Alex managed to swallow the lump of brownie in her throat. The maraschino cherries and colored sprinkles tasted good with the rich chocolate. But the texture was unusual—kind of stringy. And after that first taste, there was something else—some sharp, weird aftertaste that she couldn't identify lurking inside. "Um, well . . . These brownies are really . . ."

Gross! Alex thought as a tiny shiver shot through her. *How could you mess up brownies?*

But she couldn't say that out loud. Especially since this was no ordinary pan of brownies.

Robyn's Consumers Class was sponsoring a Teen Cuisine baking contest to raise money for a local children's charity, and everyone in the class had to bake something to enter.

At first Robyn had been bummed about it. "The only thing I know how to cook is microwave popcorn and frozen pizza," she had complained to Alex. But once she'd started experimenting with recipes, something unusual had happened.

Robyn had actually gotten excited about the contest.

Poor Robyn, Alex thought. She had this really gloomy way of looking at the world: "Expect the worst and you'll never be disappointed," she often said. So it was a pretty big deal that Robyn had thrown herself into the quest of actually *winning* the Teen Cuisine competition.

Telling her the truth would ruin things for her. It would hurt her feelings. And Robyn was one of Alex's best friends.

That's exactly why *you should tell her the truth*, Alex scolded herself. *Best friends should always tell each other the truth.*

Yeah, right, she argued back. *What about the fact that you got drenched with an experimental chemical called GC-161 on the first day of junior high school and developed special powers? What about the fact that for the past couple of years you've been able to move objects with telekinesis, shoot fireworks from your fingertips, and morph into a silvery puddle the size of a bathmat and swoosh under doorways and down drainpipes?*

How's that for being honest with your best friends?

2

Only two people in the world knew that, on the first day of seventh grade, Alex had nearly been run over by a Paradise Valley Chemical Plant truck and splattered with a secret new chemical that was being developed by Paradise Valley Chemical—the same company where her father worked as a scientist.

Her older sister, Annie—a scientific genius—knew. In fact, Alex had become her number-one science experiment as Annie worked to uncover the secrets of GC-161.

And Ray Alvarado, her best friend since preschool, accidentally walked in on them that first day in the garage and saw Alex trying out her new, weird powers.

But she'd promised Annie that, for now, it would be their secret. And besides, it wasn't as if she had actually lied flat-out to Robyn and Nicole about anything, right? She just hadn't mentioned that she could morph, zap, and float objects through the air.

Alex sighed. For now, at least, she was stuck with not telling her friends the truth about the most important thing that had ever happened in her life. So maybe she should be honest with them about the little stuff. Like Robyn's brownies.

Alex glanced at her friend. Robyn was worriedly twisting a strand of her bright red hair, waiting for Alex's verdict.

If I put down her brownies, Alex thought with a frown, *she might give up and quit! I just can't do that.*

After all, taste was relative, right? People didn't always like the same foods. For example, Alex loved chocolate ice cream—Robyn had to have strawberry frozen yogurt. Alex loved pizza with the works—her mom preferred a grilled chicken Caesar salad with that smelly anchovy and garlic dressing. Yuck!

Maybe these brownies aren't really that bad, Alex decided. *Maybe it's just me.*

"Well?" Robyn asked, her face beginning to crumple. "Tell me the truth. They're horrible, aren't they?"

"No, no!" Alex lied, smiling. "I mean, I didn't say that. They're really . . ."

Robyn looked hopeful again. "Really *what?*"

Alex searched for the right word. An answer that wouldn't exactly be a total *lie*—one that would *almost* be the truth.

A little white lie.

"They're . . ."

"Yes?"

"Interesting!" Alex blurted out. "I've never tasted anything like them!" *And that's the truth!* Alex thought.

Robyn clapped her hands. "Oh, good! Thanks, Alex!" But then she frowned again. "Interesting enough to wow the judges?" she pressed.

Alex crossed to the kitchen sink to get a glass of water, so she could rinse the odd taste out of her mouth. She felt another mild tingle shudder through her—she hoped she wasn't coming down with something. "Oh, these will wow the judges for sure," she told Robyn. *Just maybe not the way you want them to!*

Robyn sighed in relief. "I hope so. I've been having a really hard time, Alex. I've tried so many different recipes and combinations, but nothing seems to turn

4

out right. If it was supposed to rise, it fell. If it was supposed to thicken up, it turned soupy. You should have seen my first brownies—they looked like mud-pies. But with these brownies, I started to feel as if I was getting the hang of this cooking business. And I really wanted my brownies to be different."

"They're different all right," Alex said, trying not to roll her eyes.

"First, I tried my mom's recipe," Robyn went on, slicing the rest of her brownies into squares. "But it was so plain—just your ordinary chocolate walnut brownie. It was so *boring*."

Alex gulped down her water. "Boring can be good."

"Yeah, but boring won't win contests." Robyn used a spatula to move the brownies out of the pan and put them on a plate. "But then I saw this show on the Food Channel on TV. They had this really cool young chef on—he had gorgeous blue eyes and a long blond ponytail. I never knew chefs looked like that—did you? Anyway, do you know what he said?"

"What?"

"He said the best way to be an outstanding cook is to *surprise* people."

"Surprise people?" Alex repeated.

Robyn nodded. "He said people are *bored* with food. That's why they overeat. That's why they eat so much junk food. They're totally, totally bored with eating the same things day in and day out. I could really relate to that—just look what they serve in the cafeteria every day! No wonder everybody hits the dough-nut shop as soon as school lets out. So, the best chefs,

5

he said, take what's ordinary and do something crazy to it to create a—what did he call it? Oh, yeah. A 'culinary surprise.' And then people go crazy for it. That's what all the famous chefs in Los Angeles and New York City and Paris do."

"Sounds like an interesting theory," Alex said skeptically.

Robyn nodded. "So that's when I started experimenting. First, I tried adding three kinds of nuts. Then I tried adding nuts, M&M's, and coconut—"

"That sounds pretty good to me," Alex interrupted. "Maybe you should have stuck with that one."

"Nope. Still too boring," Robyn insisted. "I mean, really, Alex, you can get brownies like those at Wayne's Wigwam anytime. So then I started getting really experimental. I even tried grated carrot—to boost the antioxidant value. But finally"—she proudly held up the plate of brownies—"finally I've created Robyn's Wowie-Zowie Brownie Surprise!"

"Grated carrot, huh?" *So that's what gave it that stringy texture!* "But what exactly makes them taste . . . like this?"

"Oh, it's my secret ingredient that gives them that extra *je ne sais quoi* . . ."

"Zing?" Alex suggested.

"Yes!" Robyn smiled proudly. "It's that *zing* that makes them so different!"

"So, what is it?" Alex prodded.

Robyn grinned mischievously and shook her head. "No way, Alex. I'm not telling. It's a secret! At least until after I win the Teen Cuisine competition!" She actually began to hum as she cleaned up the counter. Alex couldn't remember ever hearing Robyn hum. She must really be excited about the contest. "But I will let you in on one of my secrets."

"What?"

Robyn held up the pan she'd baked the brownies in. "Ta-da."

Alex frowned. It was a rectangular aluminum pan, old, kind of beat-up, and black around some of the edges. "A beat-up old pan?" she asked skeptically.

"Not just *any* old pan," Robyn said. "My Grandmother Russo's pan. I barely remember her. But she was Italian, and my parents say she was the best cook in the world. With this lucky pan—and this recipe—I think I may really have a shot at winning."

"Yeah, well, good luck!" Alex said.

"Here—have another one!" Robyn thrust a brownie into Alex's hands. "You really like them? You *really* think they'll win?"

You ought to tell her the truth! Alex scolded herself. But then she wondered, *Why?* She hadn't seen Robyn this excited—and this cheerful—in ages! Why ruin it for her? Maybe the judges really would like that weird aftertaste.

Alex stared at the browie. She and Robyn had long ago sworn to be friends forever. They'd promised to stand by each other through thick and thin. The least she could do was eat a yucky brownie.

Bravely she made herself take another big bite of the brownie and forced a smile, to show Robyn just how much she liked them. "Sure," Alex told her. "I mean, why not? You've got as good a chance as anybody."

Alex grabbed her backpack from the chair by the fridge and slung it over her shoulder as she headed down the hallway for the door. "I guess I'd better be going, Robyn. I've got piles of homework to do."

"Yeah, me, too. Oh, wait! Take some brownies with you!" Robyn insisted.

"Uh, no, thanks . . . Don't you need them for the contest?"

But Robyn had already run back to the kitchen. She returned moments later with several hunks of Robyn's Wowie-Zowie Brownie Surprise in a large plastic bag. "My mom and dad are on a diet, and they hate having stuff like this around the house. I'll be making a fresh batch for the contest anyway."

Alex plastered a grin on her face as she reluctantly stuffed the brownies into the pocket of her jean jacket. "Great. Thanks. See ya, Robyn."

Alex hurried out the door and headed for home. She felt kind of rotten for not telling Robyn the truth about those weird brownies. But there was no real harm done, right? A little white lie, as her mom called them. It wasn't the same as a big fat lie told to cheat, or hurt people, or conceal bad deeds, right? It was just a tiny fib to keep from hurting her friend's feelings.

On the way home Alex spotted her neighbor, Mrs. Calavander, out spraying her large garden of red, white, pink, and yellow roses. Clouds of smelly dust filled the air as she made her attack. "Darn bugs! Take that! And that!"

Alex laughed. Mrs. Calavander had been a sergeant in the Marine Corps before she retired, and she was quite aggressive in her battle of the bugs.

"Hi, Mrs. C.," Alex called out. "Your roses are really looking good!"

Mrs. Calavander glanced up from beneath her wide-brimmed straw hat. "Oh, hello, Alex! Thank you!" she boomed through a small white mask that covered her mouth and nose. "Better not come too close while I'm spraying, though. This bug spray is mighty toxic."

Ah-choo! Alex covered her mouth and nose as she hurried past.

At the corner Alex stopped as an aging school bus chugged past, enveloping her in a cloud of exhaust. *Phew!* Alex thought, trying not to breathe in any of the fumes.

Ah-choo! Alex sneezed again.

I hope I'm not getting a cold, she thought as she came to her block. *I can't afford to miss any school right now.*

As she neared her house, she stopped by to see her best friend, Ray, who lived next door. She'd missed first period that morning because of a dentist appointment, and Ray had promised to share his biology notes with her.

She rang the bell, then heard Ray holler from upstairs, "Come on in, the door's open!"

Alex pushed open the door and pounded up the carpeted stairs to Ray's room.

Whew! The room reeked!

Ray and Louis Driscoll were hunched over a table covered with small bottles of all shapes and sizes.

9

"Alex!" Ray exclaimed with a big smile. "Just the person we wanted to see."

"What are you guys doing, Ray?" Alex asked, trying not to inhale through her nose.

"It's a scientific experiment," Louis explained. "We're trying to determine which aftershave or cologne is the most effective lady-killer formula."

Alex laughed as she picked up a bottle. " 'New, improved MAGNET will win you the girl of your dreams—or your money back.' Give me a break, guys. How can they tell lies like that and get away with it?"

"Hey, Mack, it's not a lie, it's advertising," Louis said. "So they exaggerate a little. But hey, you know me and Ray. If it doesn't work, we'll *demand* our money back."

"Where'd you guys get all this stuff, anyway?" Alex asked, sniffing a bottle.

"That one I ordered through an ad in the back of a sports magazine," Louis said, his voice dropping to a conspiratorial whisper. "It has a secret ingredient—an herb used in China for thousands of years to attract women."

Alex giggled. "Yeah, right. It smells like the 'secret ingredient' is 'eau de toilet-bowl cleaner.' "

Ray held up a bottle that looked like a miniature Egyptian mummy case. "This one—King Tut—was on sale at the drugstore."

"I guess that makes you smell good no matter how old you are," Alex joked.

"The rest of the stuff belongs to our dads," Louis said.

"Do they know you stole all their cologne?" Alex teased. Ray lived alone with his dad, and she knew Mr. Alvarado wouldn't be home from work till six.

"We didn't steal it!" Ray said indignantly. "We just borrowed it."

"Yeah, we're going to put it back," Louis insisted. "Our dads will never know."

"Now, Al," Ray said, pushing her down into a chair. "We need the female perspective. Which aftershave turns your knees to jelly?"

"*What?*"

"Yeah," Louis said. He smoothed back his curly reddish-brown hair like the leading man in a romantic movie. His goofy grin and freckles kind of ruined the effect, Alex thought. "Which one fills you with passion and longing for us?"

"Give it up, Louis!" Alex said, laughing. "It'd take a lot more than aftershave to make me swoon over you!"

"Thanks a lot, Mack," Louis grumbled.

"Come on, Al," Ray said. "Which one should we pick?"

They stuck several bottles under her nose.

"P.U.!" Alex said with a shiver. "None of them!" She hadn't meant to be so blunt, but they really stank!

"How about this one?" Louis asked. He dumped some in his hand, slapped it on his face, and stuck out his cheek. "What do you think?"

Alex started to say, "That's nice." But she couldn't—it wasn't true. "Ick!" she said. "That one's worse than all the others put together!"

11

Suddenly Alex didn't feel so good. A shiver ran through her, kind of like the chills she'd had with the flu last winter. "Uh, Ray, do you think you could open a window?" she mumbled.

But Ray and Louis were too busy opening bottles. "Try this one. It's called Knight Raider," Louis said. "Wait a minute. The stopper's stuck." He pulled, and twisted, and finally yanked it out—and spilled the entire bottle all over Alex, soaking her blue plaid flannel shirt.

"Louis!" Alex shrieked, jumping up from her chair.

"Oops! Sorry, Mack," Louis apologized. He grabbed a sweatshirt off Ray's bed and tried to dab off the spill. "But hey, at least it's the expensive stuff," he added with a laugh.

Alex didn't laugh.

"Come on, Al, don't be mad," Ray begged. "Do you want me to wash out your shirt for you?"

"No," Alex snapped, scratching her arms. "I just want to get out of here as soon as I can. Do you have the biology notes or not?"

Ray looked surprised at Alex's sudden bad mood. "Sure." He picked up a composition book from his desk and handed it to her "Here. I think I wrote down everything important. You can just give it back to me tomorrow at school. Say, how was your visit with the dentist this morning?"

"Dr. Crisman had bad breath," Alex said bluntly as she stuffed the notebook into her backpack.

Louis hooted with laughter. "Mack, I can't believe you said that!"

"Maybe you should tell him to brush his teeth!" Ray joked, cracking up.

Alex scratched her head and frowned. *Why did I say that?* It was true, sure, but it still wasn't a nice thing to say. Alex had gone to Dr. Crisman since she was a little girl, and he had always been a kind and gentle dentist. "Uh, he's really nice, though. And I didn't have any cavities. I just had my teeth cleaned and got a fluoride rinse." Alex slung her backpack onto her shoulder and headed for the stairs. She felt weird, and she just wanted to go home.

"Wait!" Louis hollered from the top of the stairs. "What about the cologne and stuff? Which one will make the girls go crazy for us?"

"Nothing could make the girls go crazy over you, Louis," Alex mumbled as she hurried down the stairs.

Darn! She hoped they didn't hear that. She didn't usually blurt out things that would hurt someone's feelings—even if it was what she really thought

Maybe it's because I'm not feeling good, she told herself. *Maybe I'm getting sick. Maybe I'm just too tired to be nice.*

Alex hurried next door to her own house. She felt like going straight to her room and climbing into bed.

But someone was waiting for her on the steps to the front door. A beautiful black cat with a white face and four white paws.

Alex quietly laid her backpack on the sidewalk and crept softly toward the porch. "Hello, sweetheart." She crouched down as silently as possible, then slowly lifted her hand toward the cat, palm down, so she wouldn't scare it off. "Hello, there. Who are you?"

The cat purred and rubbed against Alex's hand.

Charmed, Alex scooped it up and cuddled it against her cheek. "What a pretty cat you are!" She checked for a tag, but the cat didn't even have a collar. Alex knew that sometimes people would just dump a pet they no longer wanted. Could it be a stray?

"Oh, you poor thing," she said, stroking its head.

Maybe she could keep it and look after it until they found the owner. . . .

Maybe no one would claim it. . . .

Maybe she'd get to keep it herself. . . .

Alex raced into the kitchen. She'd always wanted a pet—a dog or a cat or a bird that would belong just to her. But her mom and dad always said the same thing. "Maybe next year."

Well, maybe "next year" was *this* year!

"Mom! Look what I found!" Alex called out as she hurried into the living room. "I think it's an abandoned stray! Oh, Mom, can we keep her, please, please, please—"

Sitting on the couch, blond Barbara Mack looked up from her pile of books and papers and peered over the top of her reading glasses. She had quit her job in public relations and gone back to college to get her master's degree, and it seemed as if she was always studying. "Alex!" her mom exclaimed with a frown. "You know cats make your father sneeze!" But then her frown melted as she reached out to stroke the cat's black fur. "Oh, she's adorable! She looks just like one I had when I was little."

Alex smiled hopefully. "You had a cat? What was her name?"

"Fluffy," Mrs. Mack said with a smile. "Didn't I ever tell you about her? She used to sleep at the foot of my bed. And she liked to hide among my stuffed animals." Then she sighed. "But you know we just can't keep a cat around because of your dad. I'm sorry, Alex."

Alex sighed. She remembered the last time her great-aunt—whom Alex and Annie had nicknamed Grandmack—came to visit. Alex found out that Grandmack had brought her white cat, Sir Galahad, with her, but had kept it hidden in her room the whole time so Mr. Mack wouldn't sneeze.

"Couldn't he take allergy shots or something?" Alex asked her mom. "How about if he just didn't touch the cat? I could keep it up in my room. Dad wouldn't even have to know it was there."

Mrs. Mack shook her head. "I'm sorry, honey. Maybe one day when you have your own apartment, you can have a cat. Till then I guess we'll just have to be content with the stuffed kind. I love cats, but I guess I love your dad a little bit more," she said with a grin. "Don't you?"

Alex felt another chill, and hugged the cat to her chest. "Sometimes I'm not so sure," she mumbled.

"What, honey?"

"Uh, nothing, Mom." Alex wrinkled up her nose and looked around the room.

"Alex, is something wrong?"

"What smells funny in here?"

Barbara Mack laughed. "I used rug cleaner on the carpet this afternoon when I came home from class. What you smell is the lovely fragrance of 'Country Mist Herbal Bouquet'—layered over the smell of chemical cleaners."

Ah-choo! Alex grabbed a tissue off the end table.

"Alex, honey, are you okay?" Mrs. Mack asked.

"I feel fi—" Alex began automatically, then said instead, "Actually, I feel rotten. Maybe it's the perfume in the rug cleaner."

"It *is* a bit strong," Mrs. Mack agreed. "But don't worry. The fragrance should wear off soon. I'll open a window."

"Okay, Mom."

Mrs. Mack stood up and laid a gentle hand on her younger daughter's shoulder. "Now, better get rid of the cat." She scratched it behind the ears. "Sorry, little one."

With a pout, Alex took the cat back outside and set it down on the ground. "Scoot!"

But the little cat just rubbed up against her leg as if *she* had adopted Alex. And the poor thing looked so hungry!

"All right, come on." Alex scooped up the kitten and hurried into the Macks' garage. "You can stay here for a while. Just till I can find your owners. But you've got to promise to be quiet!"

The Macks' garage hadn't seen a car in years. It was full of junk, and Annie Mack had turned one corner into her own private science lab. *With me as her biggest research project,* Alex thought.

She found an old box and put an old sweatshirt inside to make the cat a bed, then got it a small dish of milk and a can of tuna to eat.

Ah-choo! Alex wondered again if she was coming down with a cold. She hoped not. She had too much homework to do!

She played with the cat a few more minutes, then, remembering her homework, got up to leave. "See you soon," Alex said to the cat, then hurried upstairs to the second-floor bedroom that she and Annie had shared since they were little.

But just as Alex stepped through the door, she began to feel dizzy. Her knees shook. Her hair flew straight out as if she'd just gotten a perm.

Two little lightning bolts shot from her fingertips, and the lights in the room flickered as a weird shiver ran through her from her scalp to her toes.

"Alex!" Horrified, her sister Annie jumped up from her desk and quickly shut the door. "What's going on? Are you okay?"

"I don't know, Annie," Alex gasped. "But something weird is happening to me. I never felt like this before in my life!"

CHAPTER 2

"Mmm fwl howwibul!" Alex mumbled.

"Keep your mouth shut," Annie ordered her sister. "And keep the thermometer under your tongue, or we won't get an accurate reading."

Alex rolled her eyes, but did as her sister asked. Annie could sometimes get bossy with her, even though she was only two years older, but Alex knew she was just worried about her. So she clamped her mouth shut and snuggled down under the quilt Annie had tucked around her. In general, Alex was pretty healthy. In fact, she hadn't gotten sick much at all since she'd gotten drenched in GC-161 and transformed from ordinary Alex into a zapping, morphing, glowing Alex. Maybe she'd been lucky. Or maybe GC-161 would turn out to have some health benefits, like taking extra vitamin C.

Whatever. She sure was sick now.

The digital thermometer beeped in her mouth, and Annie jerked it out. "Hmmm," she said, frowning. "You don't have a temperature." She pulled down Alex's lower eyelids and stared into her eyes.

"Ow, Annie!" Alex yelped. "That's gross!"

Annie ignored her and laid her ear against Alex's chest.

"Annie, I—"

"Shhh!" Annie said. "I'm trying to listen to your heart."

"BOOM-ba-BOOM-ba-BOOM-ba-BOOM-ba-BOOM!" Alex said.

Annie sat up and glared at Alex, then carefully wrote down something in her notebook. She'd been taking careful notes ever since Alex first showed signs of her weird powers. She hoped some day in the future to publish a paper on the effects of GC-161 in the human body.

Next, Annie picked up Alex's hand and felt for her pulse, timing it against her wristwatch.

Annie looked puzzled as she dropped Alex's wrist. "Your vital signs seem completely normal. What kind of symptoms are you experiencing?"

Alex wrinkled her nose and thought. "I have a headache—not a bad one, really, just a little. Then there's the chills, and I sneezed a couple of times this afternoon. That's all. I feel tired, too. Maybe I'm coming down with a cold."

"What about the weird hair and the flickering lights?" Annie asked.

Alex shrugged. "Static electricity?" She started to turn over, but Annie laid a hand on her shoulder.

"Look at me, Alex. This is very important. I need to know everything, no matter how small or unimportant it seems. Be honest, now. Is there anything else you can tell me?"

Alex blinked as a shiver ran through her. She felt a tiny tingle in the tip of her tongue. "I really hate your shirt."

Annie stared. "What's *that* got to do with anything?"

Alex wasn't sure why she'd said it. But it was true. "You said be honest," she reminded her sister. "And I think that color looks really bad on you."

Annie stood up and jammed her hands on her hips. "That's not funny, Alex. This is serious! It's no time to fool around."

"Sorry . . ." Alex muttered.

Annie began to pace the room, her brow furrowed in thought. "I don't like this, Alex. Your symptoms are too clear to ignore. Something new could be happening to you. Something dangerous."

"Even after all this time?" Alex asked in surprise. Once she'd gotten used to the effects of the GC-161 in her system—and Annie had run a million tests—she and Annie had decided that the chemical had probably not harmed her physically.

"Maybe," Annie said. "Perhaps GC-161 breaks down in your system over time and can cause new symptoms or side effects that weren't present or apparent in the beginning. Who knows? No one's ever had such a massive amount of GC-161 in their system before."

"Oh, great," Alex said. "I was getting used to being weird and unusual—at least I knew what the rules were and I was able to control my powers most of the time. Now you're saying I may be *changing?*"

Annie bit her lip. "Look, Alex, I don't want to upset you. It may be nothing at all. But with something this unknown, we have to treat everything seriously. I better look through my notes, to see if there are any clues in the experiments we did last week." She rubbed her chin, thinking. "Maybe we should do a urine sample—"

"Annie—gross!" Alex ducked under the covers. "No way!"

Annie shook her head and patted Alex on the . . . whatever that lump was. "All right, all right. But I think you should rest till suppertime." Then she hurried over to her desk, where she dug out her notebooks of Alex/GC-161 research from a drawer.

Alex pulled the covers from her face and turned on her side. She'd gotten used to most of the side effects of GC-161, especially after Annie convinced her that she was probably going to be okay. She grinned. And to be honest—though she tried not to let Annie know—she really *enjoyed* the powers the accident had given her. Who wouldn't want to be able to morph into a puddle and sneak under doors?

But when something weird like this happened, Alex got nervous. After all, who knew what *else* GC-161 could do to her? Alex remembered the time Annie accidentally spilled GC-Divide on her while she was morphed into her puddle form. The puddle had split—and so had her personality, into a good Alex and an evil Alex. Just thinking about that made her shiver!

Had something like that happened again?

Or was GC-161 starting to play games with her insides?

Maybe the fun and games were over.

She glanced over at Annie. Her brilliant sister had on her Serious Scientist face—which meant she was concentrating so hard, she might as well be in a trance. Alex had often felt jealous of Annie's brain while growing up. But in the fix she was in, she felt really lucky to have her own personal scientist taking care of her. She knew her sister loved her and would never do any experiments that would harm her—the way Danielle Atron probably would. And she knew that Annie would never stop trying to learn as much about GC-161 as she could.

Alex shivered and scrunched down in the covers, worrying what the future held for her. And as she dozed off, she had a funny dream.

She dreamed she was playing out in the backyard with Ray, who was wearing a powdered white wig. And when his father came out, she spoke up and said, "I cannot tell a lie. I *did* chop down the cherry tree. . . ."

At dinnertime Alex felt much better. Her extremely bad hair day seemed to be over. She felt refreshed from her nap. And instead of feeling carsick, she was starving!

Alex helped Annie set the table, then slipped into her seat as her mom and dad carried in steaming dishes of food. Now that Mrs. Mack had gone back to school, things sometimes got a little hectic around the house—*especially when Mom and I have a test on the same day!* Alex thought with a chuckle.

Still, her parents were really into this family dinner thing. Whenever she could, Barbara Mack still tried to make some nice homemade kind of dinner so they could all sit down together and eat healthy foods and bond as a family. It was kind of corny.

And it was actually kind of nice.

Unfortunately, her mom also liked to experiment with foreign dishes and fringe health-food recipes, and you couldn't always guess what was in them!

Alex wrinkled her nose. *Whoa!* Something on the table really *stank!* She tried to guess which dish was the guilty one, but no such luck. Her mom apparently was in one of those experimental moods, and every dish looked as if it had been sliced and diced and given a free ride in the blender before landing in the serving bowl.

Mr. Mack chose the nearest one and cheerfully scooped a glop of something onto his plate, then passed the dish to Annie.

Annie didn't even blink. She just served her plate as if it were plain mashed potatoes, then handed the bowl to Alex.

Alex had often teased Annie that too much science

was bad for your health, and now she had the proof. *The fumes from years of scientific experiments have definitely destroyed her sense of smell!* Alex thought.

Alex tucked her long, blond hair behind her ears and leaned over to sniff the food. Yep, this was *definitely* the stinky one! What could she do? Her mom was a little touchy about her cooking. Maybe Alex could just put a tad on her plate and then clear the table quickly at the end of the meal before her mom could see that she was scraping it all down the garbage disposal. But the smell would probably ruin the taste of everything else on her plate, too.

"My afternoon class was canceled," Mrs. Mack was saying. "So I spent part of the afternoon trying out some new recipes. I figured you guys would enjoy a home-cooked meal after all the pizza and takeout Chinese we've been eating lately."

"But, Mom," Alex protested. "We *like* pizza and Chinese. Really. I could eat pizza every night."

"Oh, Alex, that's nice of you to say," Mrs. Mack replied. "But I know you guys must be feeling neglected, and I think you deserve something really nice. Besides, I really needed to work off some steam."

"How come, Mom?" Annie asked as she passed the rolls to Alex.

Mrs. Mack ran a hand through her shoulder-length blond hair. "I got accused of cheating on a test today!" she announced. "Can you believe it?"

"You?" Annie exclaimed. "Mom, that's ridiculous!"

"Of course it's ridiculous!" Mr. Mack strongly

agreed. "Your mother doesn't have a dishonest bone in her body."

"What happened, Mom?" Alex asked.

Barbara Mack shook her head. "This kid in my nine o'clock class kept looking at my test this morning. You know, dropping his pencil near my desk, pretending to yawn so he could lean toward me—really juvenile antics like that."

"So why did *you* get in trouble?" Alex asked.

"Because when the professor finally caught this guy trying to cheat, he stood up in the middle of the class and said *I* was the one cheating and *he* was just trying to tell *me* to keep my eyes on my own paper! It was so embarrassing!"

"Barbara, that's awful!" Mr. Mack said.

"What happened?" Annie asked.

"Well, we stayed after class," Mrs. Mack said. "And, of course, it was obvious from this kid's test that he hadn't studied. So that cleared things up. The professor is making him apologize to me publicly during our next class." She stabbed her fork around in her food. "I just don't understand people who cheat and lie like that."

"I hope you girls appreciate what your mother is saying," Mr. Mack lectured Alex and Annie. "People who lie are only hurting themselves. Honesty is always the best policy. Right, Barbara?"

"Right, George. Anyway, enough of my problems at school," she added with a smile. "Dinnertime should be our time to relax and enjoy ourselves after a long, hard day." She smiled around the table at her family. "So, how is it?"

George Mack looked clueless. "How's what?"

Barbara laughed. "The casserole! How do you like it?"

Mr. Mack smiled and took a bite.

He looked startled at first. Then Alex saw that look cross his face—the one that usually meant he was trying hard to figure out some scientific experiment. Alex guessed he was using the scientific method to figure out what exactly was in his mouth! "Fascinating texture . . ." he commented. "Interesting the way the two flavors remain distinct. I wonder if I could duplicate that property in the lab. . . ."

Mrs. Mack must have taken that as a compliment, because she was smiling. "What about you, Annie?"

"Um—" Annie washed down a mouthful with a slug of milk, then answered, "I think you've really outdone yourself this time, Mom."

Barbara grinned. "Thanks. It wasn't the easiest recipe. There were over twenty ingredients!"

Uh-oh. Two down, one to go. Alex's turn!

"Uh, Mom," Alex began, trying to change the subject, "did you read in the paper about those two farmers who dug up a giant sweet potato that looked exactly like Bill Clinton?"

"Come on, Alex. Try the casserole," Mrs. Mack insisted. "I need to know how you guys like it so I can decide whether or not to make it again."

Alex was cornered. She took a deep breath, picked up her fork, and scooped up a teeny-tiny bite. Trying not to breathe in the "fumes," she stuck the tip of her fork into her mouth and tasted it. *Oh, gross!* she thought in a panic. *It tastes worse than it smells!*

"Well, Alex?" Mrs. Mack said with a grin. "We're waiting for your expert opinion."

"Well . . ." Alex began, trying to be polite. She couldn't quite bring herself to lie and say it tasted good. But she didn't want to tell the truth and hurt her mom's feelings. And she also didn't want her mom to make it again, either! Maybe it was really okay. Maybe it was all those aftershave lotions and colognes at Ray's that had irritated her nose and made her more sensitive to bad smells. Maybe—

"Come on, Alex," her mother pressed. "Be honest! What do you think of the casserole?"

Suddenly Alex felt a tingle wash over her—kind of like the way her foot felt when it had been asleep and was prickling back to normal. She felt a tingling in the tip of her tongue.

And then—weird!—she felt an overwhelming, uncontrollable urge . . .

To tell the truth.

Alex ducked her head and mumbled, hoping her mother wouldn't hear.

"What was that, honey?" Mrs. Mack asked.

"Raise your chin and speak up, Alex," her father said, "so we can hear you."

Everyone stared at her.

Alex grabbed her glass and filled her mouth with milk.

"Well?" her mom repeated.

Alex swallowed. She bit her lip. She covered her mouth with her napkin.

And still she found herself opening her big mouth and saying—

"It stinks."

"*Alex!*" her father exclaimed.

Mrs. Mack looked surprised.

Annie shot her a dirty look.

"Alex," her father said with a frown, "you apologize to your mother immediately."

"Now, George," Mrs. Mack said, "it's all right. Alex has a right to—"

"She does *not* have the right to say smart-alecky things to her mother," Mr. Mack insisted.

"But, Dad," Alex tried to explain, "I didn't mean to be rude! Honest! And you and Mom just told us you want us to always tell the truth. This food *does* stink. Smell it!"

Alex glanced at Annie. Her sister gave her one of those *What in the world are you doing?* looks.

Mr. Mack looked torn. She could tell that, deep down, he agreed the food smelled awful. But she also knew he would never say so.

"That's not the point," Mr. Mack said sternly. "You were rude to your mother. And after she worked so hard to make us this lovely meal. You didn't really mean to say what you did, did you? Would you please tell her you're sorry?"

"But I can't," Alex protested.

Her father looked exasperated. "Why not?"

"Because I cannot tell a lie," Alex said. "This casserole stinks. It really smells bad—and it tastes even worse. I don't think I can swallow a single bite."

Mr. Mack's chair screeched on the floor as he stood up.

Alex winced.

Her father was not the kind of man to holler and yell. But he wouldn't tolerate anyone treating Mrs. Mack with any disrespect. He looked very disappointed as he told Alex, "Fine. If you're unable to eat a single bite of your mother's wonderful dinner, then you may be excused."

"George—" Mrs. Mack began. "Really—if she's just being honest—"

"And when we're all done," Mr. Mack continued sternly, "you can clear the table and clean up the kitchen all by yourself."

Alex stood up. *Why did I have to start a fight over something like this?* she wondered, staring at her mother's hurt, confused face. *Why couldn't I keep my mouth shut?*

"Sorry, Mom," Alex said softly. "I didn't mean to be rude or hurt your feelings. I promise."

"I know you didn't, Alex," Mrs. Mack said, a little too brightly. "Hey, I asked you to tell the truth, didn't I? I sure don't want to go to all the trouble to make this again if nobody likes it."

"But I *do* like it, Barbara," Mr. Mack fibbed. "Alex, tell your mother the truth. It's not that bad, is it?"

"But it *is* that bad, Dad." Alex tingled again. *Why am I doing this?* she wondered. *Stop it. Stop it right now!*

But she didn't. She couldn't help but add, "And I

don't think it's fair for me to have to clean up the dishes when I didn't eat any of the food."

"Alex—!"

Annie jumped up from her seat and threw her napkin down on the chair. "Uh, excuse me. I'll be right back!" Then she grabbed Alex by the arm and dragged her into the kitchen.

Alex flopped down at the kitchen table as she watched her sister run her hand through her shoulder-length dark brown hair.

"Okay, George Washington," Annie demanded, keeping her voice low so their parents wouldn't hear. "What in the world were you trying to do in there?"

Alex shrugged. "I was just telling the truth."

Annie frowned. "The truth? Alex, telling the truth is fine and dandy, but don't you think you're taking this truth business a little too far? It's not like you're on the witness stand in a courtroom here, it's just light dinnertime chitchat."

"But I can't help it!" Alex wailed.

Annie scowled. "What do you mean?"

"I can't stop myself from telling the truth!"

Annie sat down at the kitchen table and peered into Alex's eyes. "Wait a minute, Alex. Are you serious? What are you talking about?"

"I don't know," Alex said earnestly. "I really wasn't trying to be rude or anything. I couldn't help myself. When Mom asked me about the casserole, I just *had* to tell the truth."

Annie stared at her sister, thinking. "Alex," she said

slowly, "did anything else happen? Right before you told the truth, I mean."

"Well . . ." Alex tried to remember. "I did feel kind of tingly."

"When?"

"Right after Mom asked me directly how I liked her casserole."

Annie grabbed Alex's hand and stared into her eyes. "Alex, did you steal the chocolate bunny out of my Easter basket?"

"*What!*"

"Shhh!" Annie hissed, glancing through the open doorway. "You know—my chocolate bunny. When I was seven and you were five and we had that big Easter-egg hunt at Grandmother's house and Dad said I probably lost it while I was running around hunting for eggs."

Alex felt the hot blush creep up her neck like a sudden fever, and she knew she was beginning to glow like a yellow stoplight. That was one of the oddest side effects of the GC-161—and the hardest to control.

She tried to ignore the tingling in the tip of her tongue. "Why would you think that I—"

"Alex, *tell me the truth! Did you steal my chocolate bunny?*"

Alex felt the truth well up in her throat like a great big burp. She squeezed her lips together, trying to hold it in. But it was no use.

"I stole it!" she blurted. "I snuck it out of your basket when Dad was showing you that experiment that turns raw eggs rubbery by soaking them in vinegar.''

''Alex!''

''I'm sorry, Annie,'' Alex began, ''but I was only five years old, and I—''

''No, Alex, that's not what I mean!'' Annie interrupted. ''Don't you see? When I asked you a direct question, you had to tell me the truth!'' She grabbed Alex's arm and shoved up the sleeve of her striped T-shirt. ''And look at your arm.''

Alex saw the hair standing up on her arm like she had goose bumps from a scary movie.

On top of that, her upper arms were covered with a slight rash. Annie pulled down the neck of Alex's striped T-shirt. A light rash covered her upper chest.

''Annie, what's going on?'' Alex said, scratching her arm.

''Don't scratch, Alex,'' Annie said.

''But it itches!''

Annie dashed over to the fridge and grabbed the magnetized shopping list pad with the pencil on a string that her mom kept there. Then she sat down and began to scribble notes. Without looking up, she asked Alex, ''Did you have any other symptoms right before you told the truth?''

Alex thought for a moment. ''Well, yeah, I felt kind of shivery—kind of like the chills. And the tiniest tingle in the tip of my tongue. Just like when Mom asked me about the casserole!''

''And didn't you say you had some chills when you came home and felt sick?'' Annie asked.

"Uh-huh."

"Were they the same kind of chills, or different?" Annie asked.

Alex thought a moment. "I'd say they were about the same. It kind of feels like being cold and scared at the same time."

Annie scribbled some more notes. "Alex, I think we need to—"

"Annie?" her father suddenly called from the doorway. "What's going on?"

"Nothing!" Annie fibbed—the way she always had to do when it came to experiments with Alex. She tore her pages of notes off the tablet and slipped them into the pocket of her pants.

"Well, then, you'd better come finish your dinner— the one that your mother worked *so hard* on," Mr. Mack said pointedly. "The food is getting cold." Then he went back to the table.

"Hey, Annie—I didn't tell Dad the truth just then when he asked us what was going on," Alex pointed out.

"Yeah, but he didn't ask *you* a *direct question*, did he?" Annie said. "He asked *me* what was going on. How strange . . ."

"Annie, what *is* going on?" Alex asked, worried. "Do you think I need to see a doctor?"

"No!" Annie said. "We can't risk that right now— it's too dangerous. Who knows how the GC-161 would show up on an exam at the doctor's office? It could blow your entire secret!"

"But what if it's serious?" Alex wondered.

"Of course we'd take you to a doctor if it were serious," Annie reassured her. "You know that. But I don't think what you're experiencing now is life-threatening. Your symptoms are very unusual—but they're still pretty mild." Annie gave her sister a quick hug. "Don't worry, Alex. We'll figure this out after supper. Till then, try to keep your opinions to yourself!"

Alex sighed and watched her sister return to the dining room. A lot of strange things had happened to her since she'd been "showered" with GC-161. But this was one of the weirdest.

She was really scared. And that was the truth.

After supper Mr. Mack insisted on treating his wife to a movie to thank her for the nice dinner.

Left alone in the kitchen, Alex couldn't resist. Raising her hand, she wiggled her fingers at the dishes. One by one she flew them to the kitchen counter, scraped the food into the garbage disposal in the sink, then stacked the dishes in the dishwasher. She didn't even get her hands dirty.

"Alex!" Annie suddenly exclaimed.

Startled, Alex lost her concentration and her hold on the last floating dish. It began to fall—

But she dived toward the dishwasher and caught it before it could smash to the floor. "Annie, you scared me!"

"Alex, what if Mom and Dad had seen you?" Annie scolded.

"Well, they didn't." Alex filled the dishwasher with detergent, then closed the door and turned it on.

"I came down to help you clean up, since the problem at dinner wasn't really your fault," Annie said. "But I can see you don't need any help."

Alex shrugged. "I thought I should hurry so we could figure this stuff out. Annie, what's going on with me now?"

Annie led her sister upstairs to their room. "Remember when you first got sick this afternoon? I asked you if you had anything else to tell me, and then I said be honest. That's when you told me you didn't like the color of my shirt."

"Yeah, so?"

Annie closed the door to their room, then sat down on her bed—the one on the neat side of the room, with the orderly desk, the neatly made-up bed, and the polished telescope aimed out the window at the stars.

Alex sat down on the side of the room that looked like a tornado had ripped through it—hers.

"Let's do a little experiment," Annie said.

Alex sighed. She should be used to Annie's "little experiments" by now. But sometimes she got tired of feeling like a "Free Doll with Junior Chemistry Set."

"I'm going to ask you some questions," Annie said. "But try really hard *not* to tell me the truth."

"You mean, don't answer?" Alex asked. "Or lie?"

"Whatever, but no matter what, *don't* tell me the truth."

"Okay."

"First question," Annie said. "Do you like my hair?"

"What kind of question is that?" Alex hedged, feeling that burpy feeling in her throat again. And her tongue was definitely tingly. "It's fine, really, I think it's—"

"Tell the truth—do you like it?"

"Kind of boring," Alex blurted out, tingling all over. "I mean, it's okay, but I think you should really grow it out long for a change. Or chop it all off. Or maybe try a perm."

Alex clapped her hand over her mouth. "Annie! I didn't mean to say that! I—it was weird! I couldn't help it!"

"It's okay," Annie said. "And you're right. I need to try a new hairstyle, but I probably won't. Next question. I'd like you to tell me what you got me for my birthday."

Alex laughed. "No way am I telling you that!"

"See? That was a *statement*, not a *question*. No urge to tell me the truth?"

Alex waited a minute. "Nope."

"Now, let me try again. Alex—what did you get me for my birthday?"

Uh-oh, Alex thought. There was that bubble in her throat again! Quickly she stared at the glass of water on Annie's desk. She thought of showers, and rain puddles, and flowing streams.

Ka-*splish!* Alex morphed into a quivering puddle of silvery goo and sloshed under her bed. "*Ah-choo!* she sneezed into the dirty clothes and dust bunnies hiding beneath her bed. *I really need to clean up under here!*

Maybe she could slither along the wall now and slip

out under the door before Annie could grill her anymore.

"Alex!" Annie dropped to her knees and flipped up the bedskirt. "Tell me the truth! What did you get me for my birthday?"

Alex the living puddle sloshed noisily as a huge shiver ran through her. "A CD of Mozart's greatest hits," Alex gurgled. "I heard on TV that listening to Mozart makes you smarter—not that you need it. You're the smartest person I ever met."

"Thanks," Annie said with a grin. "I finally got you to admit it! Now come on out of there. You can't hide from this. We've got to figure out what's going on."

Alex flowed out from under the bed, then quickly morphed back to her regular form and flopped down on her bed. "What's wrong, Annie? Why am I doing this?"

"I'm not sure," Annie said. "Something is making you tell the truth. Your physical symptoms from this afternoon—the sneezing, the dizziness, the tingling, the slight rash—make me suspect that it's something you've ingested."

"You mean something I ate?" Alex asked.

Annie nodded. "Ate, or inhaled, or something that got spilled or rubbed on you and absorbed through your pores. Can you think of anything unusual or toxic that you've encountered today?"

"Just the world," Alex said dryly. "It's a pretty unusual, toxic place."

"Yeah, tell me about it." Annie scribbled some notes in her notebook. "At this point I can't tell whether this is some temporary manifestation, or if the GC-161 is mutating in your system to create some new side effects. I'll have to run some more tests. And you have to promise you'll report any new symptoms or side effects to me immediately, okay?"

"Okay, Annie," Alex said softly.

"And I don't have to warn you to be careful," Annie warned.

"I will," Alex said, but then she laughed. "This is pretty weird, but I guess it's not too bad. What's the worst that could happen? That I could be cornered into telling the truth? Isn't that what good girls and boys are supposed to do anyway? I mean, sure, it might get embarrassing sometimes, but—"

"Alex, don't you get it?" Annie interrupted sternly. "You're hiding one of the biggest secrets of all time— that you're the first human being ever to have been so intensely, physically altered by being drenched in GC-161! Plus, you've been living with this secret for a long time—under the same roof with *George Mack*, the scientist who was in charge of GC-161 research at Paradise Valley Chemical! What if someone from the plant finds out? What if you blurt it out at school? What do you think will happen to you? What do you think will happen to *Dad?*"

Alex gulped. Annie was right.

Something in her system was forcing her to tell the truth.

And the secret world of Alex Mack was a truth she *definitely* had to hide!

CHAPTER 3

The next morning Alex felt pretty normal.

At least, as normal as a girl who could morph, and zap, and float plates through the air *could* feel.

She wasn't sneezing. No chills. But she still had a slight rash. Luckily, it didn't itch too much.

"Maybe you shouldn't go to school," Annie said with a worried frown. "Call in sick. After all, you were having chills and, shall we say, 'unusual' symptoms? I'll convince Mom and Dad. They'll believe me."

Alex pulled on one of her favorite hats—a snug black velvet one she'd bought on her trip to Paris last summer—and burst out laughing.

"Alex, what could possibly be funny about all this?" Annie demanded.

"Don't you see the irony?" Alex said. "It's supposed

to be wrong to tell lies. But you want me to lie about being sick so I can stay at home and conceal the fact that I can't keep myself from telling the *truth*. And Mom and Dad trust you to always tell the truth, so they'll believe you if you tell them a lie."

Annie sighed. "You're right, it's kind of ridiculous. I hate all this sneaking around—especially with Mom and Dad. But what else can we do? And maybe if I tell a lie to protect you, it's an unselfish lie, so it's not as bad as if I lied for my own gain."

"Well, forget about lying for me," Alex said as she grabbed her backpack and slung it over her shoulder. "I'm doing much better in my classes this semester, and I really don't want to miss school. But don't worry," she joked. "Ray is pretty good at dodging the truth when he puts his mind to it. I'm sure he'll look out for me."

"Okay. I'll go through all my research notes and see if I can come up with anything," Annie said, then added, her brown eyes serious, "Alex, promise me you'll be careful. Remember, it's the *direct questions* that you seem unable to resist. It's highly unlikely that anyone will ask you directly if you're the GC-161 kid. But you never know. It might come out another way."

"I promise," Alex said solemnly. "And if I get cornered into telling the truth about myself, I'll . . . I'll"— she yanked the black cloche off her head—"eat my hat!"

"I wouldn't if I were you," Annie said dryly, the corners of her mouth twitching. "I hear French hats are very high in calories."

"Annie!" Alex exclaimed. "You made a joke! I'm proud of you!"

Alex ducked just as a pillow in a flowery pillowcase sailed through the air at her head.

Downstairs, Alex popped some cinnamon-raisin bread in the toaster and grabbed a juice box so she could eat on the way to school. She knew it wasn't the most nutritious way to plan for a long day of schoolwork, but she didn't want to get stuck at the breakfast table with her mom and dad.

Oops—too late.

"Morning, Alex," Mrs. Mack said, yawning as she wandered in wearing a pink nightgown and robe with a textbook under her arm. "Sit down and I'll make you some eggs or something."

"Can't, Mom, gotta go." She had to get out before her mom asked her any questions she didn't want to answer! "I, uh, have to return some biology notes to Ray." The toast popped, and she quickly smeared it with some chunky peanut butter. A little protein, a few carbohydrates, some OJ. Not bad for breakfast on the run. Then she snuck some milk into a small bowl, and headed for the door.

"Honestly, Alex," her mom said as she started some coffee. "Why would you eat a breakfast like that?"

Alex slipped out the door. "Honestly, Mom? I'm eating a breakfast like this because I'm racing out as fast as I can so that the GC-161 that has combined with some other weird substance in my system won't force me to tell you the truth when I want to tell you lies—especially that I'm contaminated with GC-161, the chemical Dad was experimenting on at work, and that I'm hiding an adorable calico cat right under your nose in the garage!"

Luckily for Alex, the door had slammed behind her. Her mom had turned on National Public Radio to hear the news. And the sanitation guys were smashing trash cans around out front. So her mom didn't hear a word.

Would Alex be so lucky the next time?

She took the bowl of milk into the garage, and the multi-colored cat came running. Alex stroked her beautiful fur as she lapped up the milk. "I wish I could hide out here in the garage with you," she murmured. She gave the cat a gentle hug, then hurried out onto the sidewalk.

Ray came bounding out of his house, stuffing his lunch into his backpack as he ran. "Hey, Al, you're early. What's happening?"

Alex grinned mischievously. "Do you really want to know? *Honestly?*"

Ray shrugged. "Sure. What's up?"

"Well," Alex said. "I cannot tell a lie."

Ray laughed. "So tell me the truth, George Washington. Did you chop down that cherry tree or what?"

"I've been exposed to some unusual substance that has interacted with the GC-161 in my system and has given me chills and a slight rash and makes me tell the truth when you ask me a direct question," Alex said.

Ray stopped in his tracks and whirled around to face her. "Say *what?*" he exclaimed. "Is that the truth?"

"It's the whole truth and nothing but the truth," Alex replied.

"Whoa! That could be lethal," Ray said. "What does Annie think?"

"She's home trying to figure out what's happening."

"What are you going to do?"

"Hide behind you," Alex said with a grin, "and dodge the truth until Annie figures out what to do!"

"Morning, Alex, how're you today?" Nicole Wilson asked.

She and Robyn were waiting for Alex at her locker before the bell for homeroom rang.

Most anybody on the planet would have simply said, "Fine. How're you doing?" But not Alex. She had to answer, "Very truthful."

Ray smothered a laugh.

Nicole smiled a little uncertainly. "Okay, guys, what's the joke?"

"It's no joke," Alex said truthfully. "I just have to tell the truth."

"That could be dangerous," Louis joked as he joined the group. "Especially in this school."

Now Ray stopped laughing. If their friends starting asking too many questions, Alex might just reveal her secret. He couldn't let that happen. "Uh, come on, Alex. We don't want to be late for class." He took her arm and started pulling her down the hall.

"Ray, maybe I ought to get my books first?" Alex suggested with a grin.

"Oh, yeah."

"So, what's this new truth thing you've got going, Alex?" Louis asked. "Is it some kind of class project? I'm glad I don't have to do it. I'd flunk!"

"It's no project," Alex responded. She stuck her head in her locker and hid behind the door as she collected her books. She was getting a little nervous here. Maybe she *should* have stayed home till Annie figured out how to fix her back to normal. "I just have to tell the truth."

"Sure, and your nose will grow long like Pinocchio if you don't," Louis said. "Come on, Mack. Inquiring minds want to know—so spill the beans."

Behind him, Ray looked like he was about to faint. Thank goodness Louis didn't ask her a direct question! Otherwise, she might have just told him everything.

But now all her friends were staring at her. What could she say? She'd better come up with some kind of explanation or they'd just keep asking—and by the end of the day there'd be three new members in the "I Know All About Alex" club. Better make up something fast.

"Okay, I'll tell you," Alex said.

Ray's eyes bugged. "B-but, Alex—"

"It's, uh . . . a bet," Alex said.

"A bet?" Ray squeaked.

Alex nodded. "Yeah, a bet. My mom and dad were giving us this big honesty lecture at home," she began, which was the truth. "And so Annie bet me that I couldn't tell the truth for one whole week."

Ray looked relieved.

Robyn patted Alex's shoulder and sadly shook her

head. "Oh, Alex, what have you gotten yourself into? This is such a deceitful world. If you try to approach it with honesty and integrity, it will just chew you up and spit you out."

"Well, I think it's refreshing," Nicole said. "The world would be a better place if everyone told the truth. Just look at our local, state, and national governments. They're run by so many dishonest politicians these days that people have begun to *expect* politicians to lie. Democracy is in danger of disintegrating right before our eyes. Don't you agree, Alex?"

Alex bit her finger as that tingly feeling washed over her. "Truthfully? No," she mumbled around her finger. "I think you're being paranoid as usual about big government and exaggerating the problem, distorting the facts. I think there are lots of honest men and women working for the government."

Nicole's mouth dropped open.

Everyone stared at Alex.

"Whoa, Mack!" Louis hooted. "Way to lay it on the line!"

Now I've done it! Alex thought.

"Thanks for being so honest about it," Nicole said sharply. "I think I'll be going now."

"Nicole, I'm sorry," Alex said, "I didn't mean—"

"No, that's fine. You're entitled to your opinion." Nicole swung her backpack over her shoulder. "But I'm feeling just a tad *paranoid* now, so I think I'll just run along to class."

Robyn followed her, but said over her shoulder,

"See, Alex? I told you. The world doesn't want your honesty."

Alex groaned and rubbed her hands over her face. Then she peeked between her fingers at Louis.

He had this goofy, moony look on his face as he smiled at Alex. Oh, no. Now what?

"Alex Mack, you know what? You're inspiring," he said, with a look of admiration on his face. "I think you've got something here. Tell the truth. Flat out." He smacked a fist into his other hand. "It's brilliant. It'll freak people out! And best of all, it's easy. No more trying to keep your story straight." Louis wandered off down the hall, mumbling to himself.

Alex groaned. "Oh, Ray, what am I going to do? Maybe I should go home."

"But what if they ask you in the office what's wrong?" Ray asked.

Alex sighed. Ray was right. Annie could have called in with an excuse. But in her current condition, Alex wouldn't be able to come up with an excuse that the office would accept. And if they asked her directly what was wrong, she'd really be in trouble. "You're right. I can't risk that. I'll just have to hang in there, and hope that Annie's figuring this thing out!"

Alex made it through homeroom okay, and she had history first period. Ray gave her a thumbs-up sign as she slid into her seat and pulled a couple of number 2 pencils out of her backpack.

Mrs. Lincoln, as tall and as thin as the sixteenth president, but without his legendary sense of humor, strode across the front of the room. The school legend was that no one had ever—in the entire history of the school—seen Mrs. Lincoln smile.

Alex sure hadn't. She was really glad her last name started with M, since Mrs. Lincoln's alphabetical seating chart put her near the back of the class. If she tried, she could usually manage to move just enough this way or that to stay hidden behind the student in front of her, even as Mrs. Lincoln marched back and forth across the room in her efforts to teach history.

"All right, ladies and gentlemen, quiet down. The bell has rung."

The class settled down, but as Mrs. Lincoln reached for her attendance book, a wave of titters and snorts washed across the room.

Mrs. Lincoln frowned, then slowly turned around. She froze when she spotted some artwork on the blackboard.

Alex gasped as she spotted what her teacher had just discovered. Someone had drawn a cartoon of Mrs. Lincoln with an *Abraham* Lincoln beard and top hat, with a cartoon balloon that said, "Four score and seven years ago, when I was your age . . ."

Alex stifled a giggle with her fist. A score was twenty years, so that would make Mrs. Lincoln about 103!

Mrs. Lincoln calmly picked up an eraser and began to erase the cartoon. "I have a lovely surprise for you all this morning," she said in her strong, firm voice. "I won't be lecturing in class today."

"All right!" some guy whispered loudly from the back.

Mrs. Lincoln glared. "Mr. Roberts, you and your fellow classmates will be delighted to learn that, instead, I am giving you a pop quiz."

Everybody groaned.

"All books and papers under your desks, people, except for three clean sheets of notebook paper. Is that gum I see back there? Let's get rid of it. *Not* under your desk, Mr. Hoffmeier, in the *trash*." She took a deep breath and rubbed her temples. "Now, since this quiz is a bit impromptu, I will read the questions aloud and allow the appropriate amount of time to answer. Please try to keep up, as I will not go back and repeat a question or give you extra time. Now, is everyone ready?"

Across the aisle, Ray shot Alex a thumbs-up and a big smile. Alex rolled her eyes and playfully crossed her fingers. She didn't mind reading about history— at least when they were learning about the way people used to live—but she really had a hard time remembering exact dates and dry facts. But she'd kept up with this unit, and she felt hopeful, if not certain, that she would do well on the quiz.

Mrs. Lincoln began with some multiple-choice questions. They were pretty easy. Then a few fill-in-the-blanks. The class period flew by.

Then came the essay questions. The first one Alex had to think about, but soon she wrote out an answer that she was happy with.

"How're you doing?" Ray whispered across the aisle.

"So far, so good," Alex whispered back.

Mrs. Lincoln's head snapped around and she stared at Alex, making her squirm. Mrs. Lincoln was merciless on cheaters, or so the rumors said. Did she suspect Alex and Ray were cheating? *Just relax and smile,* Alex told herself. *You haven't done anything wrong.*

Alex stared back, trying to convince Mrs. Lincoln with her expression that she was as innocent as a baby.

Mrs. Lincoln continued to stare at Alex as she read the final test question.

"What, in your opinion, was the worst result of the British trade invasion of China?"

Alex thought a moment. *The worst thing about the British trade invasion was that it made it into the history books so that I would have to study it for this test,* she thought with a chuckle.

Alex felt a shiver run through her. A tiny tingling in the tip of her tongue.

Oh, no!

She couldn't.

She wouldn't dare!

No way would she ever write something like that on a history test.

Not in Mrs. Lincoln's class!

She gripped her hand by the wrist. She tried to force her hand to write something lame and factual.

The worst thing about the British trade invasion was that it made it into the history books so that I would have to—

Oh, no! Alex stopped and frantically erased.

So far this weird truth ailment had only forced her

49

to *speak* the truth. But it now appeared it could make her *write* the truth as well!

She tried again.

The worst thing about the British trade invasion was that it made it into the history books—

Alex snapped her number 2 pencil in half.

I won't!

But then she picked up the pencil half with the lead. And as her loopy cursive writing filled the page, her thoughts were revealed: *The worst thing about the British trade invasion was that it made it into the history books so that I would have to study it for this test!*

"Time's up!" Mrs. Lincoln barked out.

Frantically Alex grabbed for the pencil half with the eraser. It rolled off her desk and across the floor. Alex dropped to her knees, searching for the eraser among desk and human legs.

"Miss Mack!" Mrs. Lincoln called out as the other students passed their tests to the front. "Are you all right?"

"No!" she said, then mumbled, "I'm just about to make a total fool of myself on a test!"

A few kids sitting around her laughed.

Mrs. Lincoln shook her head. "Speak up, Miss Mack."

"I—I dropped my pencil," she stammered, thankful the teacher hadn't asked her any more direct questions.

"The test is over," Mrs. Lincoln said. "Please pass your test to the front."

I can't turn this in! Alex thought frantically as she

climbed back into her seat. The bell rang, and students bolted for the door. For one brief, giddy moment Alex considered stuffing her test into her mouth, chewing it up, and swallowing it—the way spies did when captured with classified information.

But she didn't.

No way she'd be able to swallow all three pages.

But maybe she could—

A shadow fell across her test paper.

Alex glanced up.

Mrs. Lincoln cleared her throat. "Miss Mack—time's up. Your paper, please?"

Alex panicked. What could she possibly do? She couldn't turn in this test!

Then it was too late. Mrs. Lincoln reached across the desk and snatched up the test paper. Eyeing Alex suspiciously, she laid the test on the top of her stack.

Alex closed her eyes.

Her pop quiz had turned into a total bust.

I'm history! she thought with a groan.

CHAPTER 4

Alex slumped down in her seat as she watched Mrs. Lincoln walk back up the aisle. The teacher flipped the pages of Alex's test as she glanced over her answers.

Then she froze in mid-step halfway up the aisle.

She must have read page three. The final essay question.

Slowly Mrs. Lincoln turned around.

I'm toast!

"Well, Miss Mack," the teacher said slowly, "if this were English class, you'd probably make an A. . . ."

Alex blinked. *Huh?*

"Perhaps even extra credit," Mrs. Lincoln concluded. "For your wild attempt at humor." She held up the test paper by the corner, as if it were something rotten from the garbage. "Would you like to explain this?"

"No," Alex answered truthfully, then clapped her hand over her mouth.

Mrs. Lincoln's eyebrows shot up. "Too bad. Now, why did you answer this question this way?"

"I couldn't help it," Alex said mournfully. She could tell the teacher thought she was being a smart aleck.

Mrs. Lincoln glared at Alex over her half-glasses. "What do you think I should do about this?"

"Excuse it because I'm such a good kid?" Alex answered hopefully.

Mrs. Lincoln didn't crack a smile. "Usually you are, Miss Mack. I've never had any trouble from you before, although I do wish you would stop hiding in the back and participate more in class discussions. In fact, I'm quite surprised. You're Annie Mack's little sister, aren't you?"

Alex closed her eyes and sighed. "Yes. But I'm not Annie. I'm me, Alex. And *that's* who I *want* to be."

Mrs. Lincoln's eyebrows shot up. But Alex almost thought she saw her dark brown eyes soften a little behind her glasses. "Ah, Miss Mack," the teacher said with a sigh, "do you think I *like* being tough on my students?"

Alex bit her thumb as chills washed over her, as her tongue tingled with the urge to speak her true thoughts. *Don't say it, don't say it, don't say it*—

But she couldn't help it.

Her true opinion welled up in her chest—

Her tongue tingled—

And her traitorous lips spit forth the word—

"Yes."

Mrs. Lincoln's eyes snapped, and the soft look disappeared as quickly as if it had been a mirage. "Well, then, Miss Mack. Perhaps I must live up to your expectations, then. Please plan to stay after school to clean the boards and pound erasers for me."

"Yes, ma'am."

"Any more problems and you can expect a note from me to your parents. Is that understood?"

Alex nodded, then gathered up her things. She saw Ray waiting for her just outside the door, a worried look on his face.

He ought to be worried, Alex thought miserably. This was only her first class.

How would she ever make it through the rest of the day?

"Psst, hey, Alex! Nice cloud!" Keeping an eye out for Mrs. Lincoln, Robyn Russo slipped over to where Alex stood near the school's side door, pounding erasers and filling the air with a giant cloud of yellow dust.

"Hi, Robyn," Alex greeted her friend glumly.

"I heard you had a head-on collision with Mrs. Lincoln this morning. What happened?"

"Let's just say I said a few things I shouldn't have," Alex responded.

"You?" Robyn exclaimed. "Alex, you're really serious about this new honesty thing of yours, aren't you?"

Alex shrugged. What could she say? "I can't help myself. But I sure am tired of making people mad."

Since this morning, she'd just barely escaped insulting two other teachers. She'd embarrassed her English teacher by correcting her grammar. And she'd upset one of the lunch-line ladies with her opinion of the day's menu—that had nearly started a food fight!

Then she'd upset one of the most popular girls at school, Kelly Phillips, by telling her she thought the new cheers at the pep rally sounded lame. And on top of everything, she was pretty sure Nicole was avoiding her.

Robyn sighed and handed Alex her next two erasers. "What a sad commentary on modern society—when telling the truth gets you in trouble."

Alex whacked the erasers hard. "Is Nicole still mad at me?"

"I'm not sure," Robyn admitted. "She's struggling over it. You know how Nicole sees everything in terms of major issues of right and wrong. She doesn't know whether to feel as if her feelings are hurt—or to admire you for you forthright honesty. Personally, I think it'll blow over by the time she comes back from the weekend with her mom."

"Where are they going, anyway?" Alex asked.

"To Washington," Robyn said. "To visit some aunt who just had a baby or something."

Both girls laughed.

"Maybe she'll see enough dishonesty in Washington to make your truthfulness seem like pure gold," Robyn suggested.

"I hope so," Alex said.

"So, listen, Alex," Robyn said, "I wanted to ask your opinion about something."

I wish you wouldn't, Alex thought. But she said,

"Well, okay, but really, Robyn, you shouldn't let other people's opinions affect what you think."

Robyn stared at her oddly. "You don't even know what it's about yet."

"Well, I know," Alex said. "But you should think for yourself."

"But I need your help, Alex," Robyn said. "You know the dance that's coming up at the end of the month? Well"—Robyn blushed—"I'm really thinking about doing something really crazy and unusual."

Uh-oh. "Like what?"

Robyn grinned. "Promise you won't tell a soul?"

"Promise."

Robyn bit her lip and then blurted out, "I'm thinking about asking Chad Kennedy."

"Asking him what?"

"To go to the dance, silly!"

"Oh." Alex pressed her lips together and hoped that Robyn wouldn't ask her if she should do it.

"Should I?" Robyn asked, of course. "Should I ask him to go to the dance with me?"

Alex dropped the erasers and put her hand to her mouth as a strong wave of chills washed over her and her tongue tingled. She tried reciting the alphabet—backwards. She tried to remember the middle names of all her friends—anything to block the words surging to her lips.

But it didn't work. "No," Alex said, trying to keep her voice from sounding too mean.

Robyn pouted. "I know it's an unusual step for me, Alex. But I watched Oprah yesterday afternoon, and she convinced me that I needed to take a more active role in my destiny. She really got me all psyched, Alex. Don't you think I should at least give it a try?"

"No," Alex whispered.

"Why not?" Robyn demanded.

"Because I think—mmm-mmm mmmph!"

Alex whirled around and buried her face in her arms against the brick wall of the school—pretending to cough on eraser dust, hoping that would cover her words.

"Alex!" Robyn took her by the shoulder and turned her around.

"I'm sorry," Alex burst out, "but I don't think you should ask him because he'd never go out with you in a million years."

Robyn's mouth dropped open. "Well! Why don't you just come right out and say what you *really* think!"

"I'm sorry, Robyn, really I am," Alex said. "But I—"

"Never mind," Robyn said huffily as she picked up her backpack and began to walk away. "Thank you for your opinion. As cruel as it may be."

"Robyn, wait!" Alex called after her friend.

But Robyn hurried off without looking back.

Alex smacked two erasers together—hard! She was getting awfully tired of this. She couldn't wait to get home.

And Annie better have figured out how to fix me by then!

CHAPTER 5

"Think, Alex, think!" Annie said on Saturday morning in the Mack's garage.

"I'm trying, Annie," Alex said. Last night she'd told her sister all about her horrible day, and Annie had given her the bad news.

She had no idea what was making Alex tell the truth.

"As I said, this might just be some new side effect of the GC-161 breaking down in your system," Annie muttered. "Or it could be a side effect of the contamination wearing off—"

"Really?" Alex said hopefully. Wearing off? Alex could hardly remember what it felt like not to have secret powers—to be ordinary, without any extraordinary secrets. Would she be happy, or sad—or both—if the effects of the GC-161 wore off and she was plain old ordinary Alex Mack once more?

"—or getting worse," Annie added.

That was a scary thought!

"Then again, it's very possible that it's some kind of interaction with some other chemical, or an allergic reaction to something new. Think, now, Alex. Have you been exposed to anything unusual lately? Anything you might be allergic to?"

"*Meow!*"

Annie cocked her head. "What was *that?*"

"*Meow!*" Alex's stray cat poked its head up out of a basket of laundry sitting on the washing machine.

Annie put her hands on her hips. "Alex . . ."

Sheepishly Alex went over and picked the animal up. "I found her on Thursday," Alex said, cuddling the cat to her cheek. "Isn't she beautiful? Mom said I couldn't keep her, of course, because of Dad, but, well, Cat here talked me into a couple of free meals."

Annie reached up and petted the cat on the head. "She is darling," she admitted. But then her eyes flew open. "Alex! Maybe *this* could be it. Maybe you're allergic to cats—like Dad!"

Alex felt hopeful for a moment, then shook her head. "But how could I be?" she argued. "I never was before. And what about Grandmack's cat, Sir Galahad? I didn't have any weird reactions the last time *she* visited us."

"Hmmm, that's true," Annie said. "But for one thing, Grandmack hid her cat up in her room, so it wouldn't bother Dad. He didn't sneeze or anything— he didn't even know the cat was here. And you didn't really handle Sir Galahad much, either, did you? Not the way you've been cuddling this cat."

"I barely touched Sir Galahad," Alex admitted.

"Well, people who are allergic to cats are actually allergic to the dander on the cat's skin. Their symptoms occur most strongly after they've handled the cat and gotten the dander on their hands and into their eyes and nose. Maybe you've just handled this cat more—like now, the way you were rubbing it against your face. Plus, lots of people don't develop allergies until puberty. Maybe you're just now exhibiting symptoms. And then there's one other important factor."

"What's that?" Alex asked.

"GC-161. We're dealing with a chemical that no one knows much about. Its properties are a mystery, since we've only begun to study them. And I'm the only person who has studied the effects of the chemical inside a human being, and there's so much I don't know. We don't know how GC-161 might mutate or alter over time. What was true about how it affected you last month or last week might not be true today or tomorrow."

"So how do we find out if it's the cat?" Alex asked—but she was afraid she already knew the answer.

"There's only one way," Annie said firmly. "Get rid of the cat."

"Annie!" Alex cradled the cat protectively in her arms. "I can't believe you'd be so cruel—even in the name of science!"

"Alex! I didn't mean we should just ditch her somewhere! I meant we should take the cat to the animal shelter. They might even be able to find out who she really belongs to, if someone's reported a missing cat. If not, I'm sure they will see that she's adopted into a good home. Then we'll see if your rash and other symptoms disappear."

"Okay."

Annie went to ask their mom if she could borrow the car to go to the library, while Alex put Cat back into a box. Deep down, she had known she wouldn't be able to keep it. But it had been fun to keep it a while and pretend.

Would getting rid of the cat help Alex get rid of her truth troubles?

She barely dared to hope.

Mr. Mack spent the afternoon going over some research, and Mrs. Mack stayed in her room studying for a test on Monday, so there were no opportunities for Alex to insult or shock anybody with the truth. But early that evening Mrs. Mack tapped on the door to the girls' room and stuck her head in. "Hi, girls. Your dad and I are playing hooky for the rest of the night. Want to join us?"

Alex glanced nervously at her sister.

"Um, what did you have in mind, Mom?" Annie asked.

"Pizza and a movie? Your dad just ran out to rent a video, and I'm calling Sal's. What'll it be—plain cheese or the works?"

Pizza and a movie sounded great to Alex. How

much trouble could she get into if they were all watching a movie with their mouths full of pizza? Besides, maybe since Cat was gone, the truth effect was wearing off.

She looked at Annie. Annie nodded.

"Sure, Mom, that sounds great," Alex said. "How about a Veggie Supreme?"

"Sounds good to me," Annie agreed.

"You got it!" Mrs. Mack said. "I'll call you when the pizza gets here."

A little while later they were all settled in the Macks' cozy living room with a Veggie Supreme on the coffee table and a murder mystery in the VCR.

Alex loved mysteries, and she settled back to enjoy the film—a mystery about a detective investigating a murder at a dinner party.

By the end of the movie every one of the guests was a suspect. First it looked like the polo player did it.

The camera zoomed in for a close-up on the detective's face. "Did YOU do it?" he said in a French accent, staring straight into the camera.

Straight into Alex's eyes.

"NO!" she suddenly blurted out.

"Shhhh!" Annie hissed. She was so engrossed in the movie she didn't realize what had happened. Her parents didn't seem to notice, either.

Then it looked like the professor did it.

The camera zoomed in for a close-up on the detective's face. "Did YOU do it?" he cried again in his French accent, staring straight into the camera.

Alex tingled and stuffed a slice of Veggie Supreme

in her mouth, but it didn't matter. "NO!" she was forced to say.

"Alex, honey, don't talk with your mouth full," her mother said, not taking her eyes from the screen.

"Sorry, Mom," Alex mumbled.

"Did YOU do it?" the detective asked the lady in the red dress.

Alex buried her face in a throw pillow, but still mumbled, "No!"

This was ridiculous, Alex thought, and she got up to go.

"Alex," her father exclaimed, "you can't leave now. We're just about to find out who did it!"

Alex curled up at the end of the couch. Maybe if she stuck her fingers in her ears and sang "The Star-Spangled Banner" in her mind, she wouldn't hear the detective's question.

But she couldn't help it. She kept glancing at the screen—since she had to know who did it. And each time the detective accused the next dinner party guest with a robust "Did YOU do it?" Alex had to say "No."

At last the movie was over and her parents turned off the TV.

"You know, Alex," her father said, "the way you kept saying 'no' each time the detective accused someone . . . I bet you're the only one who's ever watched this movie who knew it was the *detective* who did it after all!"

"Yeah, Alex," her mother said, "how did—"

"Just don't ask me how I figured it out," Alex interrupted.

Alex and Annie helped clean up from the pizza as their dad rewound the video.

"My goodness," Mrs. Mack said, glancing at the clock. "I had no idea it was so late. Better scoot on up to bed, girls."

The girls said good night and headed upstairs.

"Annie," Alex whispered, "didn't you notice anything weird tonight?"

"Yeah, they left the green pepper off the pizza," Annie grumbled.

"No, I mean me."

"What?"

"The way I kept shouting 'No, no!' at the detective on the video?"

"Oh, my gosh," Annie said, her eyes wide as she realized what had happened. "Was that the GC-161 interaction making you say no? I was so lost in the movie, I didn't even notice."

"Well, luckily, Mom and Dad didn't think it was weird," Alex said as she led the way into their room. "And they were too busy watching the movie to ask me any direct questions. But, Annie, this is really getting to be a pain. What are we going to do?"

Annie got out some pajamas and began to change. "Don't worry, Alex. We'll figure this out. I promise. And hey, if this is caused by an allergy to the cat, maybe you'll be back to normal in the morning."

"You think so?" Alex asked.

"Sure. And if not—hey, you're so good at solving mysteries. We'll figure this one out, too."

Alex changed and climbed into bed. She gazed out her window at the full moon and wondered . . .

If Annie was so sure that everything was all right, then how come she looked so worried?

CHAPTER 6

"Alex! Get up so I can find out if you're any better,"
Annie said early Sunday morning as she sat on the
side of Alex's bed.

"I'm fine," Alex mumbled sleepily.

Annie tried again—this time with a direct question.
"Alex—how are you this morning?"

Alex pulled the pillow over her head. "Awful!"

"Really?" Annie asked worriedly. "What's wrong?"

"I've got a chirpy sister sitting on my bed trying to
wake me up on a Sunday morning when I'd rather
sleep in!" Alex grumbled from beneath the pillow.

"Ha, ha, very funny," Annie said. "Seriously, Alex.
How do you *really* feel? It's been almost twenty-four
hours since we took the cat to the shelter. Do you
think you're back to normal this morning?"

Alex sat up in bed and shoved her blond hair out

of her half-opened hazel eyes. "Annie, I don't even remember what *normal* is anymore."

"Okay. Let me rephrase that," Annie said with a half-smile. "Do you think this unusual urge to tell the truth all the time has worn off?"

Alex wrinkled her nose. "I don't know. Ask me a question, and I'll try to lie."

"Okay, what's your name?" Annie asked.

"It's Raymond—"

Annie frowned worriedly when she saw her sister shiver and turn red with the effort to lie.

"Alvarrrrrr . . . Alvar*rrrrAlex Mack!*" Alex gushed out, then she sagged against her pillow. "Oh, Annie, I tried as hard as I could to say Raymond Alvarado. But my mouth wouldn't let me!"

Annie just said "Hmmm" and went to her desk to write something down in her notebook.

Alex fought a yawn. "If it *was* an allergic reaction to the cat, wouldn't it have worn off by now?"

"How's your rash?" Annie asked.

Alex shoved back the sleeves of her pajamas. "Still there. So . . . I guess it wasn't the cat, huh?"

"Probably not," Annie answered. She pulled the covers off her sister and took her firmly by the hand. "Come on, sleepyhead, we've got a lot of work to do. We've got to find out what's giving you this bad case of brutal honesty!"

As soon as they could slip away, they headed for Annie's mini-laboratory in the Mack garage. Annie carefully cleared away some test tubes and beakers and opened her notebook. "Okay, Alex." She made what looked like a peace sign in front of Alex's face. "How many fingers?"

"Oh, Annie, is this really necessary?" Alex complained. Ever since the accident, she'd been poked and prodded and inspected—everything but dissected!—and sometimes she got so tired of it, she just wanted to morph into a puddle and slosh away from home! But Annie was all business when it came to science—especially the science of her little sister and GC-161—and she often started by checking all of Alex's vital signs, like pulse, reflexes, temperature, and vision.

"Just tell me how many fingers you see," Annie repeated firmly.

"Seven," Alex replied.

"Alex, will you please tell me how many fingers you see?" Annie said, making sure she used a direct question.

"Two—*Darn!*" Alex stomped her sneakered foot on the cement floor. "This is really getting annoying."

Annie couldn't help but laugh. "You know, this could actually be kind of fun. I could interrogate you and find out all your deep, dark secrets."

"You already know my one and only deep, dark secret," Alex shot back.

For a moment Alex just smiled at her sister in amazement. They'd been so close as little girls. They'd shared everything, and Alex remembered that they used to have the best pillow fights.

But as they'd grown older, things had changed. Annie got too "grown-up" for pillow fights. She grew more serious and more interested in science, like their dad, and the teachers loved her. Half the time she was lost in some science experiment that Alex couldn't hope to understand. Alex had often been jealous of Annie's brains, and envious of the way she seemed to connect with their dad in ways Alex couldn't.

But ever since the accident, things had changed. Alex had become Annie's number-one science experiment—the one that might eventually win her a Nobel prize or something. They'd shared a difficult-to-keep secret not only from the whole world—but also their mom and dad. Not easy! And they'd joined forces against a common "enemy"—Danielle Atron and the Paradise Valley Chemical Plant.

They'd gotten to know each other in ways they never would have if life had gone along its normal path. They'd bonded in a way that few sisters could.

All thanks to GC-161. Maybe in some strange way, Danielle Atron had actually done them a favor.

Alex sat cross-legged on top of the washing machine. "Now what do we do?"

"We'll just have to do what any good scientist does when an experiment isn't working out," Annie said.

"What's that?"

"Start over."

"Ugh."

Annie flipped to a new page in her notebook. "Okay, Alex. Let's make a list of any new materials or chemicals you've eaten, inhaled, or otherwise come in contact with since, say, Thursday night. Don't leave out anything, because even something little could be important."

Alex tried hard to remember and helped Annie make a list:

- Alex's new Strawberry Essence shampoo
- An old piece of grape bubble gum she'd found in the bottom of her pack.
- A fluoride treatment at the dentist.
- UFOs—Unidentified Food Objects in the school cafeteria
- Mrs. Calavander's bug spray
- The carpet shampoo Mom had used in the living room

"Come on, Alex, are you sure that's all?"

"I think so. Hey, you know Ray spilled almost a whole bottle of aftershave on me," Alex said hopefully. "That's definitely something I don't normally use. I bet *that* was it!"

"Could be," Annie said. "Although with chemical interactions, the amount doesn't necessarily have to be large to create a reaction. Do you think you could get the bottle from Louis so I can find out what's in it?"

"Sure." Alex jumped down from the washer. "Can I go now?"

Annie smiled. "I guess it must get tiring being a lab rat, huh? Just one thing, Alex. Remember to be careful. And if you feel you're about to reveal to anyone that you're the GC-161 kid, then do whatever you can to get out of the situation."

"Gotcha!"

Happy to escape from the "lab," Alex ran down the

driveway, leaped a hedge, and ran up onto Ray's porch.

Ray and Louis were just coming out the door.

Louis had a black eye.

"Louis!" Alex exclaimed. "What happened to you?"

"I got punched in the face," Louis muttered, "and it's all your fault, Mack."

"What? My fault?" Alex exclaimed. "What'd I do?"

Louis touched his fingertips to his eye and winced. "I was pretty impressed by this new 'honesty is the best policy' thing of yours, remember. I thought, yeah, Alex is right. After all, it's a lot easier to tell the truth all the time. Then you don't have to worry about getting your story mixed-up."

"Yeah, the way you do most of the time, Louis," Ray joked.

"Thanks, Ray," Louis said dryly. "Anyway, I've been going around telling everybody exactly what I think. No holds barred. No tiptoeing around. It was refreshing at first. Until—"

"Jimmy Hoffmeier," Ray said.

"As in Jimmy Hoffmeier the Incredible Nasty Hulk?" Alex said. "The biggest bully in Paradise Valley?"

Louis nodded. "I told him what I thought of the way he picks on kids half his size. And he showed me what he thought of my opinion."

"It was ugly," Ray commented.

"So now," Louis went on, "I'm going back to my old motto: 'Why tell the truth when a little white lie makes everybody happy?' "

"Wish I could do that," Alex mumbled.

"Ah, sure you can, Mack, it's easy."

Not for me, Alex thought. "So, Ray, I was wondering. Could I borrow that cologne of yours—you know, the one Louis spilled all over me?"

"Knight Raider?" Louis asked. "Say, Mack, you might do better attracting guys if you wear *women's* perfume."

Ray looked puzzled. "So what do you want it—"

He broke off as he saw Alex wildly shaking her head. He looked puzzled at first, then seemed to get it.

No questions!

"That's okay, you don't have to tell me why you want it," Ray said.

But since he hadn't asked her a question, Alex could say whatever she wanted. "Annie and I want to borrow it to see if we should get it for Dad for his birthday," she fibbed.

"Knight Raider?" Louis exclaimed. "For your dad? Maybe you better try something tamer!"

"I can't loan it to you anyway," Ray explained. "After Louis spilled it, I threw out the bottle. When I told Dad about it, he said not to worry. It was a real old bottle anyway. He said they don't even make it anymore."

Alex frowned. That was rotten luck.

"So, you want to play a little basketball?" Ray asked.

"I guess so," Alex said. If she went home, Annie would just want to poke her and test her some more. Maybe a little game of hoops would cheer her up.

Ray got his basketball and the three walked over to a nearby park to shoot baskets. *It's pretty easy, hanging out with Ray and Louis,* Alex thought. They didn't ask too many questions. Maybe that was the best kind of friend to have.

Then Ray and Louis decided they wanted to go see a movie, but Alex had already seen it, so she headed home.

"Alex!" her mother called out crossly as soon as she came in the front door. "Where have you been?"

Alex tossed her hat on the living room couch and hurried toward the kitchen. Barbara Mack was a pretty terrific mother. True, she and Alex didn't always agree, but Barbara was usually a pretty cheery person.

Alex pushed through the kitchen door—and gasped. The place was a wreck! Bowls and boxes and egg cartons crowded the kitchen table and countertops. The refrigerator door had handprints on it. Alex took a step forward and felt her athletic shoe squish into some gooey spill. "Mom, what's wrong?

Mrs. Mack sighed and rolled her eyes heavenward. "Danielle!"

"Danielle Atron?" Alex frowned. Her mom had once worked at a public relations firm that had Paradise Valley Chemical as a client. Danielle had often sent their mother into a raging tizzy over projects for the company. But now that she had quit and gone back to college, Barbara rarely saw her.

"I don't get it, Mom," Alex said. "You don't work for Ms. Atron anymore. What's the problem?"

"The problem is that your *father* still does!" Mrs. Mack complained.

Alex laughed as Annie blew a stray strand of dark brown hair out of her eyes and rubbed her nose with a floury hand, leaving a white smudge on her flushed cheeks.

Annie shot Alex a strange look—a mixture of irritation and worry. "Guess what?" she muttered.

Alex stuck her finger in Annie's bowl of chocolate batter. "What?"

Mrs. Mack picked up a wire whisk and began to attack another bowl. "Danielle called your father into work today. Sunday—can you believe it? Apparently some potential Japanese investors are in town to observe Paradise Valley Chemical's operations, and Danielle insisted that George come in to explain his GC-161 research to them."

Alex made a face and hopped up onto the one clean area of the kitchen counter. "So what's that got to do with cooking?"

"Your father," Mrs. Mack said pointedly through gritted teeth, "invited them to dinner. At our house. Tonight. And guess who gets to cook?"

Alex jumped down from the counter. "Oh, no! Mom—" She exchanged a worried glance with her sister and whispered, "Annie!"

A look that said: *Danielle Atron—in this house—now, when Alex couldn't tell a lie?*

"Uh, why didn't you tell him no, Mom?" Alex exclaimed. "Why don't they just go to a restaurant?"

"Don't ask me!" Barbara said huffily.

"I tried to get her to do some kind of takeout or catered food," Annie said. "But you know Mom . . ."

"Well, I can't help it," Barbara said. "Especially after George repeated what Danielle said."

"What?" Alex asked.

Mrs. Mack put on this real fake cheery face and said, " 'Oh? Barbara cooks?' " She began to beat her batter again, and her eyes gleamed. "I'll show her 'Barbara cooks.' Maybe I should make them that casserole that I made you guys last Thursday. Then maybe she'd get an idea of what I really think of her!"

Alex and Annie exchanged a look—then all three Mack women burst out laughing.

"I'm sorry, girls," Mrs. Mack said, giving each girl a quick hug. "Thanks for putting up with me while I let off a little steam. I'm really not mad at your dad. He's a kind, generous man, quick to offer his hospitality, and I'm sure he was just trying to be friendly to foreign visitors. That's why I love him. And I'm sure we'll all have a lovely time."

"Not!" Alex and Annie said together.

"By the way," Mrs. Mack said, "I'd appreciate it if you girls would dress up a bit, for your dad's sake."

"But, Mom!" Alex exclaimed. "Do Annie and I *have* to be here?"

"Of course," Mrs. Mack said. "At least for the dinner part. Your father expects you to be here."

"But—but—those dinners with people from the plant are so boring," Alex tried to explain. "And— I've got homework. Right, Annie?"

Annie was nodding.

"Lots and *lots* of homework," Alex went on.

Mrs. Mack shook her head as she leaned over to check something in the oven. "Alex, your father and I have asked you over and over not to leave homework till the last minute on Sunday night. Now, you've been out all day hanging out with your friends. It won't hurt you to spend a little time doing this for your father. It's very important for him to make a good impression on these people. And if they do decide to invest in the company, it would mean more money for your father's research. Wouldn't that be wonderful?"

Alex and Annie exchanged a glance. "It sure would," Annie said.

"Besides," Mrs. Mack went on, "it should be lots of fun to meet some visitors from Japan. You'll probably learn a lot. Maybe you could even do some kind of extra report for school—for history or social studies."

"But, Mom—"

Mrs. Mack held up a hand for silence. "Alex, you can do your homework after supper."

Alex recognized that voice. It wasn't a loud voice, or a mean voice. But Alex knew that when her mother used that voice, it was no use to argue.

Mrs. Mack went to the broom closet and pulled out a feather duster. "Here's your magic wand, my dear. Now, scoot—go make the dust in the living room disappear! And we probably need to vacuum, too."

"Okay, Mom." Alex took the duster and headed toward the living room. But behind her mother's back she signaled for Annie to follow her.

"Um, I'll be right back," Annie said, wiping her hands on her apron as she followed Alex.

"Well, hurry, Annie," Mrs. Mack said. "We've still got a lot to do."

"Annie, what am I going to do?" Alex whispered frantically when she and her sister were out of earshot.

"Now, Alex, calm down," Annie said. "Maybe it's not as bad as you think."

"What do you mean?" Alex exclaimed. "I might as well just turn myself over to Danielle Atron the minute she walks in the door."

"Maybe not," Annie replied. "You know how Danielle is. She's always so self-absorbed. Really, Alex, she's not likely to ask you a lot of questions. You're a kid. In fact, she's more likely to ignore you."

"Maybe," Alex said as she began to dust the furniture, but she wasn't convinced.

CHAPTER 7

"Konnichi wa," Mrs. Mack said warmly late that afternoon as her husband led Danielle Atron and their Japanese visitors—one young woman, one young man, and one older, grouchy-looking man—into the Mack living room.

All three bowed slightly at the waist and repeated her greeting: *"Konnichi wa,"* or "good afternoon."

Danielle Atron, dressed in an expensive-looking teal business suit, smiled a practiced smile and said, without warmth, "Hello, Barbara. So good to see you again."

"I'm glad you all could come," Mrs. Mack replied.

Alex was impressed with how polite and friendly her mother could be toward someone she really disliked. And she was proud of how her mom had pulled things together with so little notice. The living room seemed cozy and inviting. The dining table was set beautifully, with nice dishes and fresh flowers. Soft classical music played in the background.

Was it lying to be nice to someone you couldn't stand? Alex thought as she watched Danielle brush off the couch before sitting down.

Then she remembered something her mother had always told her when she'd come home from elementary school complaining about a classmate she didn't like: "You don't have to like everyone," her mother had said. "But you do have to be nice to everyone."

Alex smiled as she saw her father give her mother a quick hug. "Everything looks wonderful, Barbara. Thank you."

"I was glad to do it—for you," Mrs. Mack whispered back, then grinned. "Of course, *you'll* be cleaning up the kitchen, won't you?"

"Absolutely!" Mr. Mack said.

Mrs. Mack grinned back. "I promise to keep you company."

Mr. Mack introduced Alex and Annie to their guests. Mr. Yamaguchi and Mrs. Ikejima smiled and said hello. But the older man, Mr. Nishimura, merely nodded with a stony face, as if he wished he were still in Japan.

Alex and her sister hurried into the kitchen. Their mom had given them the choice: sit and chat with their guests or serve hors d'oeuvres and dinner.

The girls had quickly chosen to serve. No way did they want to sit and chat with Danielle—when Alex couldn't keep the truth about herself to herself.

"So far, so good," Alex said as she and Annie began to put food on the trays.

"As long as nobody asks any questions, you'll be fine," Annie reminded her. "If you suspect anyone's about to ask you something, just drop an hors d'oeuvre and run to the kitchen for something to clean it up with!"

"Good idea."

Annie picked up a tray of stuffed mushrooms, crackers with weird toppings, and spinach dip.

Alex didn't understand people her parents' age. With so much good stuff to snack on, why did they always have to go to so much trouble to make these icky little vegetable thingies that nobody could tell what they were?

She wrinkled her nose as she picked up the tray of sushi—vinegar-flavored rice garnished with bits of raw seafood. Mrs. Mack had learned to make it in a "Food 'Round the World" cooking course at the Y. Not only was it a favorite food in Japan, but it was also becoming a popular hors d'oeuvre in the United States. The sushi looked really pretty, but Alex didn't think she could eat raw fish. "Why couldn't we just have chips and dip? Or nachos?" Alex complained.

"Come on, Alex, eat one," Annie said. "I'm sure you'd like it if you tried it."

"No way," Alex exclaimed. "This fish is so raw, it's still moving!"

Annie chuckled and led the way to the living room, where they walked around, serving the food as the adults chatted. Their Japanese guests spoke fairly good English, and Mrs. Mack's warm, genuine smile seemed to put them at ease.

"I'll have sushi," Danielle said, reaching for Alex's tray. She took several pieces and placed them on her plate, then turned back to Mr. Yamaguchi. "As I was saying . . ."

Excuse me, Alex wanted to say sarcastically. *In this country it's polite to say "thank you"!*

Alex turned around quickly—and the last piece of moist sushi slid off her tray. Without thinking, Alex used her powers of telekinesis to freeze it and scoot it back on the plate.

Aaaaggh! Why'd I do that! She glanced around. Most of the adults were deep in conversation with Mr. Mack. *Nobody saw me,* she told herself nervously. *Probably.*

"Excuse me."

Alex turned around at the sound of the soft voice. Mrs. Ikejima frowned slightly as she said in heavily accented English, "May I ask question?"

Ohmigosh! Did she see me move the sushi? Alex wondered. She shot a look at Annie, who shook her head. *No questions!* she mouthed silently.

"Actually, I'd better go to the kitchen—"

"Wait!" the woman exclaimed urgently, laying a hand on Alex's wrist.

Oh, no. Now I've done it, Alex worried. *I wonder how you say "Can you keep a secret?" in Japanese?*

She saw the woman dig in her purse. But what she pulled out surprised Alex.

A thin black wallet.

Mrs. Ikejima unsnapped it, flipped it open, then held it out. Alex saw a picture of a young Japanese girl with long dark hair and a pretty smile. "My daughter, Satsuki. I promise her I bring back gift." She pointed at Alex's outfit. "Some American clothes she would like. Can you tell me a store of clothing young girls like to go?"

Whew! Alex smiled. "Sure. I'll write down the name and directions for you before you leave."

"*Arigato gozaimasu*," Mrs. Ikejima replied with a slight bow. "Thank you."

Alex wished she knew how to say "you're welcome" in Japanese. Instead, she said "You're welcome," and tried to imitate the woman's gentle bow.

Alex made it through the rest of the hors d'oeuvres without a problem. But she was still nervous about the dinner part.

"Don't worry," Annie whispered as they moved toward the dinner table. "Just keep your head down and play the shy, quiet, old-fashioned daughter. If we're lucky, Danielle will be her usual self, which means she'll hog the conversation and no one will pay us any attention."

Alex giggled as she started to sit down next to Mrs. Ikejima. It might be fun to ask her questions about her daughter Satsuki and what teenagers in Japan were like.

But Danielle brushed past her and took the seat, so she'd be between Mrs. Ikejima and Mr. Yamaguchi.

"Alex," Mrs. Mack said with a smile. "Why don't you sit here, next to Mr. Nishimura."

Oh, great, Alex thought. *I get to spend the evening with Mr. Grouch.* She sighed and took her seat. Mr. Nishimura nodded curtly, then turned his attention back to the others. *Well,* Alex thought, *at least he's not likely to ask me a bunch of questions.*

Soon everyone was seated and passing food around the table. Mrs. Mack hadn't attempted to compete with cooks back in Japan. Instead, she had decided to prepare for her foreign guests a traditional American meal: meatloaf, mashed potatoes, steaming corn on the cob, and hot yeast rolls. Alex thought it was delicious, and their guests seemed to be enjoying the meal as well.

Mr. and Mrs. Mack were good hosts and tried to keep the dinnertime conversation light and entertaining. Alex enjoyed hearing the mixture of English and Japanese. Perhaps if she listened closely, she could learn a few words before the evening was through. But Danielle kept forcing the conversation back to business and the Paradise Valley Chemical Plant.

That made Alex nervous, and she found herself counting the minutes till she and Annie could clear the table and go to their room.

Just then Alex saw her father search the table. "Would anyone care for horseradish? I love it on meatloaf."

"I'll get it," Alex quickly volunteered. She ran into the kitchen, but took her time finding the small jar of horseradish in the fridge. She waited as long as possible, trying to spend as much time away from Danielle as she could. At last she went back, knowing her dad would come looking for her if she didn't return soon.

"Here you go, Dad." Alex set the small jar next to his plate.

"Thanks, sweetheart." He opened the jar and spooned a huge glob onto his meatloaf.

Whew! Alex thought. It had a sharp smell that made her nose burn.

"Care for some?" her dad asked.

"No, thanks!" Alex replied.

But just as she returned to her seat, she heard Mr. Yamaguchi ask a question that struck fear in her heart.

"But, George, what about the rumor we have heard?"

"What rumor is that?" Mr. Mack asked between bites of meatloaf.

"That there is a child free in this town—who has been contaminated with a large dose of GC-161?"

Danielle Atron's eyes flashed, but she plastered on a beauty-pageant smile. "Why, that's just a nasty old rumor. It's been going around for years." She laughed. "It's almost become a town legend, like Paul Bunyan and Johnny Appleseed."

"Johnny . . . who?" Mrs. Ikejima asked, puzzled.

A muscle twitched in Danielle's cheek. "Never mind. The point is, there is no child."

"I tend to agree with Danielle," George Mack spoke up. "If some poor child had been exposed to GC-161 in large amounts in uncontrolled circumstances, he or she would probably exhibit such a strong reaction that any good parent would have noticed. Then the parents would surely have taken the child to a doctor or emergency room, and the medical personnel would have contacted our plant for information about the truck involved in the accident, as well as the chemical substance that had contaminated the child. However, in all this time, no one has ever come forward."

George Mack gazed fondly at his own two children. "I'm a father, and I will tell you, I worried about this for a long time. I can't imagine what it would feel like to have such a horrible accident happen to one of my children."

Alex and Annie exchanged very guilty looks.

Then Alex laid down her fork and dropped her eyes to her plate. Hearing her father speak like that! George Mack's worst nightmare *had* happened to one of his own children—*her!* Suddenly it seemed hard to remember why it was so important to lie about it to her father and mother. Perhaps she should just tell him. He'd know what to do.

And yet, think how it might hurt him to learn that the chemical he had helped develop had altered his child?

She'd have to talk to Annie about that soon.

Danielle propped her elbows on the table and laced her fingers. Her blood-red nail polish gleamed in the candlelight. "Well, I for one am sure it was all just gossip. Aren't you, George?" she added, her eyes informing him of what she wanted his answer to be. Alex guessed she feared that any hint of scandal would scare off their investors.

Alex's father missed the look entirely, but nodded

his head in agreement. "I feel certain someone would have come forward by now. I mean, after all, why hide it? I'm sure the child's parents would insist on seeking medical treatment. They would probably even want to sue the company for endangering their child's life."

Danielle grimaced, and George yelped as if someone had kicked him under the table. Alex guessed it was the pointed toe of Danielle's expensive leather pumps. When everyone looked his way, including Danielle, Mr. Mack laughed faintly and said, "Ooops. Must have bumped my knee on a table leg."

But then Mr. Mack went on. "It used to worry me when I thought some kid might be hurt. I've studied small amounts of GC-161 in the lab, and I can't imagine what it would be like to be so totally soaked in the chemical under nonscientific conditions." He glanced at Alex and Annie. "You're familiar with our experiments, Annie. Can you imagine what it would be like to be the GC-161 kid the rumors have described? How about you, Alex?"

Annie gasped.

Alex froze.

She tried biting her lip as her tongue tingled and her deep, dark secret welled up inside of her.

"Yes," Alex whispered, trying to keep her voice quiet as the truth forced its way to her lips. "I can."

Barbara Mack knocked over her glass. It smashed onto her plate, spilling ice and water all over the tablecloth. There was a lot of noise and confusion as she jumped up, dabbing at the mess with her napkin. "Oh, clumsy me!" Mrs. Mack said, a little too woodenly. "Annie, will you help me clean this up? Then we can have our cake and coffee in the living room."

No one seemed to be paying any attention to Alex. Except for Mr. Nishimura.

He turned toward her, his cold, stern expression sending chills deep into her bones.

But even that couldn't stop her from finishing the fatal words she had started to say: "And the reason I can imagine is that I *am* the GC-161 kid that everyone has been looking for."

CHAPTER 8

Alex felt paralyzed. She broke out in a cold sweat.

Well, say something, she silently begged Mr. Nishimura.

Then she noticed him staring strangely at her.

Alex stared back, terrified.

"Hmmmm?" Mr. Nishimura said, shaking his head.

Oh, no! He'd asked her to explain! Alex struggled in vain to stop the words from passing her lips. When the words forced themselves out, she tried to whisper, so at least only Mr. Nishimura could hear. "I said I'm the GC-161 kid. On the first day of junior high school, a truck almost ran over me, hit a hydrant, and then this huge barrel of gold gunk spilled all over me."

"Ah?" Mr. Nishimura said, his eyes wide.

"It's true," Alex said helplessly. "And now I have

the weirdest side effects, such as being able to morph into a puddle and move objects with my mind. That's called telekinesis, did you know that?"

Mr. Nishimura shook his head and mumbled something brief in Japanese. *"Iie, wakarimasen."*

Oh, gosh, what did that mean? Alex wondered frantically. She laid a hand on his sleeve and peered into his dark brown eyes. "Oh, please, Mr. Nishimura. You won't tell anyone what I just said, will you? It might get my dad in trouble."

He shook his head again and repeated more loudly, *"Iie, wakarimasen!"*

Now it sounded like a threat. Was it some ancient Japanese challenge?

Suddenly a hand landed on Alex's shoulder, and she jumped.

Slowly she turned around.

"Excuse me," Mrs. Ikejima said with a slight bow. "But Mr. Nishimura—he say, 'I don't understand.' He no speak English. Nothing. Would you like me to translate what you say for him?"

Alex sagged against her chair in relief. He couldn't speak English? Then that meant he couldn't possibly have understood her confession! "No, thank you," she was able to answer truthfully. "I would *not* like you to translate." Quickly she jumped up from her chair. "Why don't you go sit down in the living room? I'll see if I can help my mother."

She dashed into the kitchen. But now she had another problem. Had Barbara Mack understood what

Alex had said? Was that why she knocked over her glass?

"It was the only way to stop the conversation." Alex heard Mrs. Mack explaining her big spill to her father. "You kept talking about the GC-161 kid and parents suing—honestly, George," she said, stifling a giggle. "I thought Danielle was going to blow a gasket!"

"Gosh," Mr. Mack said, shaking his head. "Thanks, Barbara. I was just speaking my mind. I didn't realize I'd said too much."

Barbara wiped a smudge of horseradish off his cheek with the tip of her apron. "That's okay, dear. That's why I love you. Because you're as open and honest and straightforward as a child."

Not this *child,* Alex thought sadly.

"Thanks, honey." George frowned. "I think."

Barbara laughed. "Yes, it's a compliment, George. Now, let's go join our guests." She slipped her arm through her husband's and led him into the living room.

Alex collapsed into a kitchen chair.

"Alex!" Annie whispered. "What happened?"

"Well," Alex choked out, "you know when Dad asked us if we could imagine what it would be like to be the GC-161 kid?"

Annie gulped. "Uh-huh?"

"I answered."

"What!"

"I confessed everything to Mr. Nishimura."

"Alex! Oh, no!" Annie began to pace the cheery

kitchen. "Let me think, now. There's lots of ways we can handle this. We can—"

"Annie, it's okay!" Alex grabbed her sister by the shoulders and laughed. "Guess what? Mr. Nishimura doesn't speak English!"

"He doesn't speak English?" Annie gasped out. "None?"

"Not a word."

The girls hugged and swung each other around.

"He doesn't speak English!" they crowed.

"Shhhhh!" Barbara Mack poked her head into the kitchen. "Girls—remember we still have guests."

"Sorry, Mom," Alex apologized.

"Ready to serve the cake?" Mrs. Mack asked.

"Mom, I'd be glad to serve the cake and coffee myself," Annie said. "And I had a question I wanted to ask Mrs. Ikejima, too. Alex really does have a lot of homework. And it's math." She crossed her arms and shook her head. "And you know how much extra study time Alex needs in math! I don't mind, really."

"Well, okay," Mrs. Mack said and gave Alex a quick hug. "Thanks for helping out tonight."

"No problem," Alex said, smiling. *At least, not anymore!*

Mrs. Mack hurried back into the living room, and Annie picked up the tray of chocolate cake slices on dessert plates.

"Thanks, Annie," Alex said. "Except for the part about how terrible I am at math!"

"Hey, it worked, didn't it?" Annie said with a grin.

"Now, don't make a liar out of me—go on upstairs and study!"

Alex smiled and fled up the stairs.

She'd made it through the worst truth trap she could imagine—dinner with Danielle. Things couldn't possibly get worse . . . could they?

CHAPTER 9

"Class, I'd like you all to welcome our visitor today, Officer Rivera from the Paradise Valley Police Department. He's the department's new drug and alcohol education officer. I'll let him explain." Alex's teacher, Ms. Nielson, led the students in applauding their guest.

It was Monday afternoon, Alex's last class. With Ray's help, she'd managed to avoid, dodge, or escape every difficult situation of the day. She hoped Annie would figure out something soon.

"Hey, kids," Officer Rivera was saying. "I'll be visiting your classroom on a regular basis to talk with you about the dangers of drugs, alcohol, and tobacco. We'll also be doing some role-playing, and talking about ways you can deal with peer pressure."

Officer Rivera held up a sheaf of papers. "I want to

start off today by giving you all a four-page questionnaire to fill out. It's anonymous, so just put your age and whether you're a boy or a girl. We want you to be completely honest. You see, I don't want to just rehash what you learned in grammar school about drugs and alcohol. You guys are young adults, and we want to do some straight talk in here, about the real world and the things you're really concerned about. This questionnaire will help me find out what kids in Paradise Valley know and don't know, and if there are any problems that we need to deal with. That will help me understand better how to talk with you. Okay?"

Officer Rivera handed out the questionnaires. "Remember now, this is not a test or anything—there's no 'right' answer. Just write down what you think or feel."

Alex glanced over the questionnaire. It seemed easy enough. *A lot easier than Friday's history test*, she thought with a chuckle. She figured, since all the questions were written down, she was home free.

Let's see, number one.

Which has more alcohol?
a. an 8-ounce beer
b. a 4-ounce glass of red wine
c. a 2-ounce shot of vodka.
d. They all have the same alcoholic content.

Alex knew the answer to that: d.
Number two: *How many alcoholic beverages would a*

driver have to consume to be declared legally drunk in this state?

The class was quiet as everyone worked on their answers. Alex scratched unconsciously at the rash on her arm as she flipped to the next page and found that the next questions allowed the kids to fill in their own answers.

Have you ever tried cigarettes, cigars, or chewing tobacco? If so, at what age, and what was your experience?

No, Alex wrote, then went on to the next question. The thought of chewing tobacco made her stomach churn.

Have you ever tried an alcoholic beverage? If so, what, and at what age?

Alex started to write *No*, but then, she realized that wasn't entirely true. When she was five years old and a flower girl at her mother's college roommate's wedding, she and Annie had stuck their fingers in a glass of champagne and tasted it. Yuck—they'd hated it! She remembered how they had gotten a big lecture from Dad about *never* tasting *anything* if you didn't know what it was. She and Annie had cried and cried. But she *did* catch the bride's bouquet!

Alex laughed softly. That was probably not exactly the answer that Officer Rivera wanted. But hey, it was the truth!

Alex glanced at the clock. She'd better hurry. The final bell would ring soon, and school would be out for the day.

Hey, wait a minute, Alex thought, flipping over the

last page. She only had three pages of questions. Didn't Officer Rivera say there were four?

She raised her hand. "Excuse me, Officer Rivera? My questionnaire only has three pages. Am I missing a page?"

"Sorry about that. Yes, you should have four pages. I tell you what, I'll just read you the final question, and you can write your answer on the back of the last page."

"Great, thanks," Alex said. She smiled at him and raised her pencil, ready to write.

Officer Rivera picked up his copy of the questionnaire and flipped to the last page. "Ah, here we go." He smiled, then read the question out loud to Alex. "Have you ever taken or been exposed to any illegal, recreational, or otherwise experimental drugs or chemicals? If yes, what, and what was your experience?"

Alex nodded and glanced down at her paper to write. *Of course not,* she thought. She started to write *No.*

But instead she found herself writing the word *Yes.*

What! Alex scribbled out the answer and tried again.

Have you ever taken or been exposed to any illegal, recreational, or otherwise experimental drugs or chemicals? Officer Rivera had asked her. *If yes, what, and what was your experience?*

Alex shivered and once again tried to write *No.* But then she gasped as her hand began to write a cursive *Y.*

Alex trembled with dread. She knew what was happening. Officer Rivera had asked her a direct question, and she could not help herself. She had to write the truth—the whole truth—and nothing but the truth.

Yes.

Alex lifted her pencil from her paper. She tried to sit on her hands. She tried to stuff them into the pockets of her jeans.

But she couldn't fight it.

She had to write the truth.

On the first day of junior high school, I was involved in an accident with a truck from the Paradise Valley Chemical Plant. I became drenched with the experimental chemical GC-161, which company CEO Danielle Atron is illegally trying to develop as a diet drug that will allow people to pig out as much as they want without getting fat.

I immediately developed special powers—telekinesis (the ability to move objects with my mind), the ability to morph into a silvery puddle of goo and travel under doors, the ability to create force fields and stop bodies in motion, and the ability to shoot electrical charges from my fingertips— I call it zapping.

My sister Annie has been doing experiments on me and hopes one day to publish her research, but for now we have kept my GC-161 contamination and my secret powers a complete secret from everyone, including our parents, Mr. and Mrs. George Mack—since Dad works at Paradise Valley Chemical. Well, my best friend Ray Alvarado knows, too.

Alex stared at her paper.

I can't believe I wrote this! she thought. But of course, she could believe it. Because it was the truth.

And Alex Mack couldn't tell a lie.

I can't turn this in! Alex thought frantically. This was a thousand times worse that the history test answer. But if she didn't turn in something, Ms. Nielson and Officer Rivera would wonder what she was hiding! Then she'd be under scrutiny anyway.

Officer Rivera did say the questionnaire was anonymous. It didn't have her name on it. So the police wouldn't know she wrote it, would they?

But Ms. Nielson knows your handwriting! Alex reminded herself. *And you just wrote down the names of your parents, your sister, and your best friend.*

It wouldn't take Sherlock Holmes to figure out who she was.

Even though the questionnaires were supposed to be anonymous, the incredible information she had written would be too important to ignore. The police would be able to trace her questionnaire to her parents, and her secret would be revealed. She and Annie would have no control over how the information was announced to the world.

Oh, Annie! she thought helplessly. *What do I do?*

Alex glanced around, desperately wondering how to avoid turning in her questionnaire.

Maybe she could just ball it up and not turn it in!

But then they'd want to know why.

Maybe she could just tear off the last page and not turn that in.

Maybe she could—

"Time's up!"

Alex jumped. Officer Rivera was standing right behind her.

He smiled at Alex. "I'll take that."

"But I—"

Too late!

Officer Rivera snatched her paper—with its incrimi-
nating answer—right off her desk!

CHAPTER 10

Alex's hands trembled.

But not with chills from the GC-161 plus whatever that was coursing through her veins.

Alex trembled in fear.

She'd nearly been caught many times before. She and Annie and Ray had managed to wiggle their way out of many tight spots that could have wound up with Alex as Danielle Atron's GC-161 lab rat.

Now she had confessed the entire truth—to a police officer.

How long till they traced the questionnaire back to her?

What would her parents say when they learned of the remarkable secret she and Annie had kept from them for so long? Would the government shut down Danielle Atron's illegal operations? And what would happen to her father? He was completely unaware of Danielle's secret plans for GC-161. Would she take her former top GC-161 scientist down with her?

Alex couldn't bear to imagine.

Riiiiiiiiiiiiinnnnnnnnnggg!

Classmates grabbed their books and backpacks as they stampeded for the door.

But Alex just sat there, feeling hopeless.

Ray came over and sat in the empty desk in front of her. "Al, what's wrong? You look like you've just lost your best friend. But that can't be," Ray said, flashing her favorite smile, " 'cause here I am."

Alex quickly told Ray what had happened.

Ray's smile instantly vanished. She had never seen him look so scared. But then he grabbed her hand and squeezed it tight. "Don't worry, Al," he reassured her, and his smile reappeared. "Hey, we've been in worse trouble before, right? And don't I always get you out?"

Alex laughed out loud. What would she do without good old Ray? "But that's only because you usually help me get into trouble in the first place!" she teased him.

"Come on," Ray said, pulling her to her feet. He glanced at the front of the classroom, where Officer Rivera was just putting all the questionnaires into a worn leather briefcase. "We'll just follow Officer Rivera," Ray whispered. "Leave it to me. Somehow we'll figure out a way to get that questionnaire back."

Alex nodded, but she was worried. They had often snuck around to foil the attempts of Paradise Valley

Chemical's creepy ex-security chief, Vince. They'd even managed to elude Lars, the suspicious new European scientist that Danielle had hired, supposedly to help her dad in his GC-161 research.

But following an officer of the law and trying to steal a piece of paper out of his briefcase? *Yikes! That was a new one!*

Officer Rivera strode out the classroom door, and Alex and Ray moved to follow him.

"Oh, Alex!" Ms. Nielson called out. "Can I speak to you for a minute?"

Alex whirled around. "Uh, I'm kind of in a hurry today, Ms. Nielson," she stammered. "Could I—"

"This will only take a minute."

Alex turned back to Ray, her eyes frantic.

"Don't worry, Al," Ray assured her. "I'll follow Officer Rivera and try to stall him or something." He punched her gently in the shoulder, then dashed out the door.

Alex hurried over to her teacher's desk.

"Yes, Ms. Nielson?"

Ms. Nielson was a new teacher, young and earnest. She glanced down a moment, tucking her shoulder-length blond hair behind her ear as she rearranged some paper clips on her desktop.

Please don't ask me any weird questions! Alex begged silently.

"I don't mean to pry into your privacy, Alex. It's just that—" Ms. Nielson seemed to search for words. "You usually seem like such a—a happy person. But the last class or two you've seemed . . . distracted. Or troubled." Ms. Nielson's soft, green eyes searched Alex's face. "I just want you to know, Alex, that . . . well, a lot of the teachers at this school really care about you kids. If you ever feel you need someone to talk to—about anything—I hope you'll feel free to come to me. Or one of the other teachers, or one of the guidance counselors. We really can help."

Alex felt an odd catch in her throat. It was the nicest thing any teacher had ever said to her. And oh, how she longed some days to just tell some grown-up everything—so that maybe they could fix it, or make the problems go away.

But today was not the day.

"Is there anything you'd like to talk about?" Ms. Nielson asked shyly.

Thank goodness she phrased her question that way! Alex thought in relief. "No," she said, shaking her head. She *did* have a problem—but she really *didn't* want to talk about it!

Ms. Nielson's brow furrowed. She seemed anxious to say more. But she didn't. She just nodded and added, "Well, my door's always open, okay?"

Alex smiled gratefully. "Thanks, Ms. Nielson. That's nice to know. Maybe I'll take you up on that one day." She slung her backpack over her shoulder and headed for the door. "See you tomorrow!"

As soon as she was out the door, she searched for Ray. As usual, the halls had emptied quickly as kids escaped from school into the freedom of the afternoon.

Nowhere. Ray was nowhere to be found.

She ran to the school's entrance and down the front steps.

There! He was in the faculty and visitors parking lot, standing next to a black-and-white police car, talking to Officer Rivera. Thank goodness! She couldn't imagine what Ray had been talking about all this time with a policeman!

Ray glanced nervously toward the school. Alex waved, and Ray nodded slightly. Officer Rivera had his back to the school and didn't see her.

Quickly Alex ducked behind some shrubbery near the parking lot. She took a deep breath to relax, then imagined herself diving into a swimming pool in the middle of summer. She'd learned early on that images of water helped her morph.

Soon a familiar tingle washed over her, and then she felt herself sinking as she liquefied into a silvery, gooey puddle.

Hoping no one would notice, she shot out from behind the bushes and across the brief section of grass before sloshing onto the asphalt of the parking lot.

Scratchy, she thought as she slithered to the black-and-white police car. She much preferred grass or carpet.

"So, uh, that's why I was kind of thinking that it would be cool to be a police officer when I grow up," Ray was saying.

Oh, brother! Alex thought with a laugh. She wondered how many years you could get for lying to a police officer about your career aspirations! Of course, Ray changed his mind about what he wanted to do just about every week, so who knew?

"That's just fine, son," Officer Rivera responded. "I have to get back to the station now, but I'll tell you what I'll do. I'll send Ms. Nielson some information about careers in law enforcement. Maybe she'd even like to arrange a tour of the police station for your class."

Ray's eyes bugged out as he saw Alex slither up the side of the police car at a door to the backseat and slip in through a window that was cracked open a couple of inches. "Uh, that would be, um, great—*super!*" he answered, recovering quickly. "I'm sure everyone in the class would enjoy that, sir."

Officer Rivera went around the car and opened the driver's side door. "Well, thanks for your interest. So long!" Then he climbed into the car and started the engine.

Alex stifled a gasp as she felt the car rumble to life. *Wait!* she begged silently. She had just reached the officer's briefcase lying on the backseat, but she still hadn't managed to open it.

"Uh, thanks a lot, Officer," she heard Ray say, leaning in the driver's side window, trying to stall the policeman.

"You're welcome, Ray," Officer Rivera replied.

Alex concentrated, and morphed back into her normal form, careful to crouch down low on the floorboard. She hoped Ray's conversation and the staticky announcements on the police officer's CB would cover the sounds of her movements.

"Uh, Officer Rivera," Ray said loudly, "can I ask you one more question?"

CLICK! Alex snapped open the clasp on the briefcase.

"I'm sorry, Ray, I really have to go now."

Alex's heart pounded in her chest as she quietly hunted through the stack of questionnaires.

"But, sir—" Ray begged, holding onto the window.

Officer Rivera laughed. "I'm delighted you're so enthusiastic, Ray, but I've really got to go or I'll be in hot water with the sergeant! See you!" He rolled up his window and waved good-bye.

Alex still hadn't found her questionnaire, and her hands were trembling so hard, she was having trouble flipping through the papers.

Alex saw Officer Rivera lower his head as he searched his glove compartment for something.

There! She found it! She grabbed her questionnaire, then—

Officer Rivera sat up, now wearing a pair of mirrored sunglasses. He paused and glanced over his shoulder into the backseat.

But Alex had morphed back into a puddle just seconds before, and she lay quietly underneath his seat, where he couldn't see her. Her questionnaire had morphed with her.

Shrugging, Officer Rivera turned back around and released the parking brake.

With Ray no longer distracting him, would he spot her if she tried to slip out the window now?

But before she could decide to make the move, the police car drove off!

It looked like Alex was going for a little ride down to the station house!

CHAPTER 11

Alex felt a familiar tingle shudder through her as Police Officer Rivera drove through the quiet tree-lined streets of Paradise Valley. She wondered frantically what to do.

She never knew exactly how long she could remain morphed—but she had a feeling her time was about up!

Just then she felt the police car come to a stop. Officer Rivera opened the car door and got out. She heard his bootheels click on the pavement as he walked away.

Seconds later, Alex couldn't help herself.

She felt herself morph from goo to girl in about five seconds flat.

Alex crouched down on the floor of the car and listened.

She heard other people chatting and car doors slamming. Where was she? And where was Officer Rivera?

Slowly, carefully, she peeked over the front seat so she could see out the front window.

Gas pumps. With a hand-printed sign that read:

PLEASE PAY INSIDE BEFORE PUMPING GAS

—MARK

I know where we are! she thought. Mark's Mini Mart.

Officer Rivera must have stopped for gas on the way back to the station. She waited till she saw him stride into the mini mart to pay.

Now was her chance to get out—but she had to hurry!

Quickly Alex opened the back door facing away from the entrance to the store. She hoped no one would notice her. People might feel the need to question a kid secretly climbing out of the backseat of a police car!

Staying hunched down, she scrambled toward a nearby pay phone and quickly picked up the receiver. "Oh, really? You don't say!" she said as an operator said in a nasally voice, *"If you'd like to make a call, please hang up and try again. If you need help, please hang up and then dial your operator."*

Just then Officer Rivera came out and began to pump gas into his police car.

Alex faced the phone. Would he recognize her from class? There was no reason she shouldn't be here, an innocent teenager making a phone call after school. But she'd just as soon he not notice her at all.

A few minutes later she heard the engine rev up, and then the car drove away. When she was sure he was gone, Alex hung up and fell back against the phone, sighing in relief. She was glad that was over!

"Hey, Al!"

Alex turned and spotted Ray racing toward her. He stopped when he reached her, dropped both his backpack and hers to the ground, then bent over his knees, gasping for breath.

"Ray, are you all right?" she asked.

"Yeah," he gasped out. "Followed . . . police car. Ran . . . all the way. Did you get your questionnaire?"

Alex held it up. "Got it! But I was afraid he was going to catch me and haul me in! Thanks for stalling him till I could get away from Ms. Nielson, Ray. Otherwise, the whole truth about me would be on its way to the police station right now." Impulsively she threw her arms around him and gave him a big hug.

"Whoa, hold it!" Ray protested, still out of breath. "If you *really* want to thank me, you can buy me something to drink!"

"You got it!" Alex said as they headed for the mini mart door. "What'll it be: seltzer, sports drink, or soda?"

"How about one of each?"

"You got it!" Alex said. "Just as soon as I tear this questionnaire into a hundred thousand tiny unreadable pieces!"

CHAPTER 12

The next morning Alex woke up.

She felt funny.

She sat up and spotted her sister sitting at her desk in her robe, writing furiously.

"Annie—quick! Ask me something!" Alex cried.

Annie jumped up from her desk and hurried over. "Why? Do you feel different?"

"Yeah, kind of funny . . . I don't know. Just ask me something so I can try to lie."

"What state do you live in?"

"Rhode Island!" Alex exclaimed happily.

"Wrong!" Annie cheered.

"Quick—ask me another one," Alex demanded.

"How old are you?"

"I'm two-hundred-and-forty-seven!" Alex declared happily. "Oh, Annie! I'm fixed! Whatever was wrong with me is over!" She hugged her sister, but then noticed that Annie had stopped smiling. "What's wrong?" Alex asked. "Isn't this what we wanted?"

"Of course, Alex," Annie replied. "Only . . . your body seems to have completely eliminated all traces of whatever it was you ingested. I guess it took about four days. But now we'll never know for sure what caused it."

Alex couldn't believe what her sister was saying. "Who cares? I'm okay now—that's all that matters."

"But what if it happens again?" Annie asked.

"What if doesn't?" Alex leaped out of bed and hurried to get dressed. She actually looked forward to going to school today, now that she had some control over what she said!

"Well, I'm going to try to get a sample of GC-161 from the plant and mix it with some of the items on your list," Annie said. "Then maybe I'll have some answers."

"Whatever floats your boat," Alex said. "I'm just glad the whole thing is over."

A worried frown crept over Annie's face as she watched Alex bound out of the room for breakfast.

"Oh, Alex, I don't think this 'thing' will ever be over," she whispered, "as long as your body is full of GC-161."

"I think I've died and gone to heaven!" Ray exclaimed that afternoon in the school gym.

Ray, Louis, Alex, and Nicole were trying to decide

between chocolate-macadamia nut cookies, pineapple upside-down cheesecake, and cherries jubilee popcorn.

It was the afternoon of the Teen Cuisine competition, and the principal had let all students out of their last class twenty minutes early so they could attend. The contestants had been asked to prepare one batch of their recipe for the judges, and another batch to sell to raise money for the local children's charity.

"I just know I'm not going to win," Robyn said, fiddling with the edge of her apron. "There are too many entries. Did you see Kelly's fabulous five-layer coconut cake? It looks like it was baked by Martha Stewart."

"Maybe it was," Nicole said. "Kelly's such a cheat."

"Come on, Robyn," Alex encouraged her friend, "don't be so pessimistic."

"Oh, it's much safer this way," Robyn said. "If I lose, I'll already be depressed, so it won't matter. If I win, it'll be like winning the lottery."

"So," Ray said, smiling flirtatiously, "you sure look lovely today, Robyn."

"I agree," Louis said. "In fact, I've never seen you looking more radiant than you do to—"

"Forget it," Robyn said. "No free samples."

"Aw, come on," Louis begged. "Lunch in the cafeteria was awful today. I'm starving!"

"Give me a break, Louis," Robyn said. "It's only a quarter! And it's for charity."

Louis and Ray dug in their pockets as Nicole dropped a quarter into a paper cup and picked up a brownie.

"How about you, Alex?" Robyn said. "I know you love my Wowie-Zowie Brownies. Come on, it's for a good cause."

Alex tried not to make a face. The last thing she wanted was another of Robyn's brownies. But what could she say without hurting Robyn's feelings? "Okay," she mumbled, and handed over her quarter. Ray bought three.

Nicole took a bite of her brownie and smiled.

Don't tell me she really likes them! Alex thought.

But when Robyn bent over to check her purse for change, Nicole made a disgusted face, turned around, and politely spit the bite of brownie into a napkin. "Uh, delicious, Robyn! Too bad I'm on a diet—I could eat a dozen of these."

Alex narrowed her eyes at Nicole, and Nicole shifted uncomfortably.

Louis had seen her, too.

"How about you, Louis?" Robyn asked, holding out a brownie on a napkin.

"Uh, no, thanks," he said uncomfortably. "I just decided I'm more into cookies today. See you guys later." And he hurried off to search for something different.

Ray just stood there chewing, his eyes glazed over in dreamy delight. "I love absolutely *anything* with chocolate," he murmured.

Huh? Alex thought. *Ray really likes them? Hmmm, maybe Robyn changed the recipe.*

Relaxing, Alex scarfed down her brownie. Mmmm,

her mouth filled with the delicious taste of cherries and chocolate and sprinkles and—

Ewwwww! The aftertaste hit her all of a sudden. That same ingredient—whatever it was—was still in the recipe. "Wowie-Zowie" was right! How could Ray eat these?

Suddenly Alex got a weird, tingly feeling—like she was coming down with the chills.

The hair prickled on her arms.

Her hair stood out like it was full of static electricity.

"Uh, Alex!" Ray gasped. "Come here—quick! I've gotta ask you something in private! We'll be right back, guys!" And, with that, he dragged Alex out into the hallway.

Alex scratched her itchy arms as the overhead lights flickered.

"Alex!" Ray said. "What's happening?"

"I don't know, Ray," Alex moaned. "I'm having a relapse. My symptoms are back! Ohhh, don't tell me I've got to go through all this truth stuff again!"

"But why's it happening again?" Ray wondered. "Why here, and why now?"

Alex's eyes suddenly popped open. "Robyn's brownies."

Ray shook his head. "How can you think of eating at a time like this?"

"No, Ray, I mean it must be Robyn's brownies! There must be something in those brownies that's causing a weird reaction in me. I've got to find out what she put in them!"

"Well, you'd better stuff your hair under your hat before you go back in," Ray said. "It looks weird."

"Good idea." Alex stuffed her wild hair into her green crocheted hat. "Come on, Ray. I've got to find out what's in those brownies!"

Back at Robyn's table, Alex tried to act as if she loved Robyn's Wowie-Zowie Brownie Surprise. Maybe that way she could weasel the recipe out of Robyn.

"So, Alex, what do you think?" Robyn asked, nervously twisting the ends of her apron sashes. "Don't you just love my brownies? Do you think I'll win?"

Oh, Robyn! I wish you hadn't asked me that! Alex stuffed another brownie in her mouth to stop the truth from welling up in her chest. *No, no, please no!* she thought.

Maybe she could control it—tell the truth but make it come out in a way that wasn't too mean. Mind control—that was it. *Say "I can tell you put a lot of love—and a lot of chocolate—into your brownies!"* she ordered her mind. *Say "I'm sure the judges will notice them! Wowie-Zowie—what a great name for brownies that taste like this!"*

But when she opened her mouth, none of those little white lies came out. "No," she blurted. "You can't win because your brownies taste awful!"

Alex gulped as she stared into Robyn's startled blue eyes. *Yep,* she thought, *my "truth" problem is definitely back—and as strong as ever!*

"Alex!" Nicole exclaimed. "I can't believe you said that. How could you be so cruel?"

Please don't ask me any questions! Alex thought

116

glumly, then was forced to answer, "Because it's the truth, isn't it? You hate them, too."

A guilty look crossed Nicole's face. "Now, Alex," she said with a nervous laugh, "why would you say that?"

"I wish you hadn't asked me that," Alex squeaked, trying to avoid saying what she knew she would say: "I can tell you hate them because I saw you make a face, then spit yours into a napkin when Robyn wasn't looking!"

"Nicole!" Robyn exclaimed. "You didn't!"

Nicole shot Alex a look that could burn a hole through metal. "Well, Robyn, actually, I did. But it isn't what you think!" she insisted as Robyn's face scrunched up into a pitiful pout. "I told you, I'm on a diet."

"Really?" Robyn asked. "I bet you're just saying that to make me feel better."

"No, it's the *truth!*" Nicole insisted, then winced. Alex could tell Nicole was uncomfortable telling flat-out lies.

But Robyn just folded her arms and plopped down in her chair. "I knew it."

Ray shrugged. "Hey, they taste fine to me."

"So what?" Robyn snapped. "I've seen you in action in the cafeteria, remember? You'll eat anything!" She stared at her brownies as if they were cockroaches. "I may as well quit and go home now. No way do I have the slightest chance of winning."

"Wait, Robyn, you can't quit now!" Nicole exclaimed.

"Come on, Robyn," Alex pleaded. "Don't give up. It doesn't really matter what we think. What's important is what the judges think."

Robyn just turned up her freckled nose and refused to answer.

"I'm sorry I hurt your feelings," Alex said, trying to soften the blow. "But I'm your friend. You want your friends to tell you the truth, don't you?"

"Not really," Robyn sniffed. "In fact, I'd much rather have my friends tell me a nice, fat lie!"

Nicole glared at Alex as she put her arm around Robyn and patted her reassuringly on the back. "Alex, this is all your fault."

Alex took a deep breath. This wasn't going to be easy. But she had to know what was in those brownies that was having this outlandish effect on her!

"By the way, Robyn," Alex asked, trying to sound as nice as possible, "can I, uh . . . have your recipe?"

Both her friends stared in shock.

"Are you kidding?" Robyn shrieked. "D-did you hear what she just asked me?" she asked Nicole. "She totally insults my cooking—then asks me for the recipe!"

"Alex, that's really lame," Nicole said sternly.

"But I really, really need it," Alex begged. "Please let me have it?"

"No way, Alex," Robyn replied. "Not in a million years!"

CHAPTER 13

There was only one thing to do.

Alex tossed a dollar on the table. Then she grabbed several thick brownies, wadded them up in a couple of napkins, and stuffed them into her backpack. "Thanks!"

"Hey!" Robyn cried, jumping to her feet. "What do you want with my brownies if you hate them so much!"

But Alex didn't wait to answer. She glanced around, hoping that none of her teachers would notice, and dashed out of the gym. Officially school was out for the day, and Alex had attended the Teen Cuisine event. She just couldn't wait around for the judges to announce the winners.

She and Ray ran all the way home. As soon as they reached the Mack house, they stormed into the kitchen, where they found Annie making herself a cup of decaffeinated raspberry tea.

She nearly dropped her cup. "What in the world—?"

"My symptoms are back!" Alex shouted. She spread the slightly mashed brownies out on the kitchen table. "There!" she exclaimed, pointing at the offensive blobs of chocolate. "Something in there is forcing me to speak the truth!"

"Brownies?" Annie exclaimed. She shook her head. "But, Alex, you've eaten brownies hundreds of times since your accident, and you've never—"

"But, Annie, these are different!" Alex cried. "Robyn insists she made them with a secret ingredient using her grandmother's lucky pan. As soon as I ate one of her brownies, all my symptoms came rushing back." She shoved up the sleeves of her maroon knit shirt. "See?" she said, scratching her upper arms. "My itching's back. And, oh, boy!" She dropped down into a chair next to Annie. "You should see Robyn and Nicole—they are both so mad at me."

"Told some truths they didn't like, huh?" Annie asked.

Ray rolled his eyes. "I've never seen them so mad."

"Alex, did you or did you not pay me back that ten dollars you owe me?" Annie demanded.

"Say *what?*" Ray exclaimed with a puzzled look on his face.

"It's a test, Ray," Annie explained.

Alex sighed. "I didn't." She'd been hoping her sister

might just forget that she owed her that money. "*Now* do you believe me?"

"Okay, Alex, I believe you. But are you sure these brownies are what made you develop your truth symptoms again? Did you eat anything else at the bake-off that might have—?"

"Nothing," Alex insisted. "Only this. I'm sure it's the brownies."

"Yeah," Ray said. "You should have seen her. Her hair stuck out all over the place like she'd been electrocuted or something!"

Annie sniffed the brownies. "I can smell something unusual—a sharp note over the familiar dark chocolate smell." She sniffed again, then broke off a small piece, picked off the cherry, and tasted it. She shuddered and wrinkled her nose.

"It's awful, isn't it?" Alex asked.

Annie frowned. "Not awful, exactly. It starts out tasting like a regular brownie, but then when you swallow, it's got this sort of aftertaste . . . a sort of zing! I can't figure out what it is. How about you, Ray? Did you taste the brownies?"

Ray nodded. "And I guess they do taste a little different, but I didn't think they were gross."

"Yeah," Alex said, rolling her eyes, "but that's coming from a guy who eats hot sauce on scrambled eggs!"

"Ewwww!" Alex and Annie exclaimed together.

Ray laughed. "Hey, you girls don't know what you're missing."

Annie sat back in her chair, thinking. "And you're sure Robyn won't reveal the ingredients?"

"Annie, I don't think Robyn's *ever* going to speak to me again about anything, much less tell me how she makes these brownies!" Alex said. "Is there any way you can figure out what's in them? You know, maybe drop a little chunk into a few test tubes and see which ones bubble?"

"I don't know, Alex. It's not that simple. I don't really have the equipment for something like this; I might be able to send it off to have it analyzed, but that could take a while. . . . ."

Just then the front door opened and they heard Mr. Mack call out, "Hi, kids, I'm home!"

Alex and Annie exchanged a surprised look. Their father never came home this early!

Mr. Mack strolled into the kitchen, looking at the mail. "Hi, girls, hi, Ray."

"Dad, what are you doing home?" Annie asked.

"Oh, I took our Japanese friends to the airport, and Danielle told me I didn't need to come back to the office today. I think she was really pleased with how well we entertained our guests on Sunday—though, of course, she'd rather die than come right out and say it." Mr. Mack chuckled, then glanced at the kitchen table. "Oh, brownies! May I?" He picked up a brownie and took a big, fat bite. "Mmmm. Delicious!" He opened the refrigerator and took out the milk. "But don't tell your mother. She really doesn't like us eating sweets before dinner."

Alex and Annie exchanged a glance. "You *like* the brownies?"

"They're great!" Mr. Mack said. "But then, I absolutely love anything with horseradish in it." He chuckled. "Never heard of horseradish brownies before, though. It really gives them a certain . . . zing!"

"Horseradish!" Alex, Annie, and Ray exclaimed at the same time.

"Dad—are you sure?" Annie asked.

Mr. Mack nodded. "Oh, yes. The taste is unmistakable—especially to a horseradish aficionado like myself. Did you girls make them?"

"Uh, no," Alex said, "Robyn did."

"Well, tell her I think they're delicious." Mr. Mack paused to take another bite, staring at the ceiling as he chewed and swallowed. "You know, you might tell her, though, that these might be even better if she tried using fresh-grated horseradish instead of the kind in the jar." He poured himself a glass of milk. "Well, thanks for the snack. I'm going to go check the news on TV."

As soon as he'd gone into the living room, Alex, Annie, and Ray burst into laughter.

Horseradish!

"Now, wait," Annie said, "we've got to be scientific about this." She hurried to the refrigerator and dug around until she came up with a small jar of prepared horseradish. "Ray, grab a spoon. Alex, come on upstairs. We've got an experiment to do!"

Upstairs, behind closed doors, Annie dug the spoon into the small jar of wet, white stuff and held it out to Alex. "Here, Alex. I hate to ask you to do this, but it's important to know for sure." Then she sat down at her computer. "I'm going to go on-line and see what I can come up with."

Alex sniffed the soggy white condiment. "Phew! What is this stuff, anyway? It smells sweet and bitter at the same time."

"It comes from a root, sort of like ginger," Annie explained as she tapped into the World Wide Web.

"It smells sharp," Alex said. "And yet, it almost smells kind of sweet, too."

"Just taste it, Alex."

"Okay, Annie. Anything for science—and your one-day-to-be-famous GC-161 research. Just promise me you'll dedicate your Nobel-prizewinning paper to me."

"Little sister, you got it."

Alex wrinkled her nose and stuck the tip of the spoon in her mouth and took a bite of pure horserad-ish. "Yech!"

They waited a moment, watching for signs.

Alex scratched her arm.

She shivered.

Her tongue began to tingle.

And then her hair stood out—whoa!—like she'd been electrocuted.

Annie nodded, scribbled something in her notebook, then abruptly asked, "Alex, have you ever told Ray a lie?"

Alex clapped her hand over her mouth. "Mmm-hmm," she mumbled.

"Al! Say it isn't so!" Ray exclaimed. "When?"

Alex ducked her head. "When I told you I liked the way you played the saxophone."

Ray laughed. "That's okay, then. I'm terrible at the saxophone. Thanks for trying not to hurt my feelings."

"But, Annie," Alex said. "There's something I don't understand. That first day, when I ate the brownies at Robyn's, the effects came on gradually. I didn't really realize anything was wrong till I got home. That was about forty-five minutes to an hour after I ate it. How come the effect is so much more dramatic now?"

"I'm not sure," Annie said. "It may be that even though the symptoms seem to have subsided, you still have traces of the horseradish-GC-161 interaction in your system. So when you ate the brownie this afternoon, and the straight horseradish just now, your reaction was stronger and quicker. Plus, people with allergies often become more sensitive to the offending substance with each attack."

Annie clicked on the keyboard and pointed at the computer. "Look at this, guys!"

Alex and Ray looked over Annie's shoulder at the screen.

" 'Horseradish,' " Alex read aloud. " 'One of the five bitter herbs of Passover, along with nettle, horehound, lettuce, and coriander.' It says the flavor is overpowering, so use sparingly."

"Yeah, tell me about it," Alex said.

Annie scanned down the page. " 'Avoid putting in aluminum pans, as this may cause some reaction and alter the taste or discolor the pan.' Hey, what kind of pan did you say Robyn cooked those brownies in?''

"Her lucky one," Alex said, then her eyes lit up. "An aluminum one. I saw it!"

"Maybe there was some kind of reaction between the horseradish and aluminum, which then reacted to the GC-161," Annie muttered, lost in thought. "I could probably recreate that in the lab."

Annie started to close the document, when suddenly Alex grabbed her hand. "Wait a minute. Look."

Alex began reading a section with the heading FOLKLORE. She scrolled down the document, just skimming the information. "Whoa. I don't believe it! Look at this!"

Annie and Ray leaned in for a closer look.

"One folklorist wrote her master's thesis on several traditional uses of foods and herbs in one tiny area of the Appalachian Mountains. One seemed to be based on the belief that horseradish could induce truthfulness. During the time of a full moon, young girls would bake it into cakes or pies for their sweethearts, hoping to induce them to tell the truth and, hopefully, declare their true love."

"That's what happened to you," Ray said. "Except for the part about declaring your true love."

"But I did eat horseradish—and then I told the truth. And hey! It was a *full moon* Saturday night."

"That's right," Ray said. "I remember."

But Annie laughed. "You guys can't be serious. Alex, this story's just an old wives' tale. A superstition. It's not true."

"How do you know, Annie? I ate horseradish—and I told the truth, didn't I?"

"But, Alex, Ray, that's—that's ridiculous!" Annie sputtered.

"No more ridiculous than a chemical called GC-161 making me zap electrical flashes from my fingertips," Alex argued.

"But, Alex, there's absolutely no scientific proof that such a thing ever actually occurred. Just a paper from some grad student trying to think up some obscure new topic to write about."

"Maybe I'm your scientific proof."

Annie threw up her hands. "Believe what you want, Alex. But I'm putting my money on the horseradish-aluminum-GC-161 chemical interaction. I believe you had a strong allergic reaction to the new combination it created. It makes a lot more sense."

"Well, just because something makes sense doesn't mean it's true."

Alex and Annie smiled at each other as an unspoken understanding passed between them.

They'd grown so close these past few years, and yet they would probably always look at the world a little differently.

But, hey, thought Alex. *That's what makes being sisters so interesting!*

That night, when Alex and Annie went downstairs to say good night, they found their parents laughing at an old black-and-white show on a vintage-TV channel.

"What's going on?" Alex said as she leaned over the couch between her parents during a commercial.

"This woman is taking her boyfriend to meet her father, and everything is going wrong," Mr. Mack explained, laughing. "Like, she's made sandwiches to eat on the way, and it turns out the guy is allergic to the horseradish she put on them."

"So he breaks out in these huge, itchy, red blotches right before he meets her father," Mrs. Mack said. "It's a hoot."

"Really?" Alex exclaimed innocently. "From horseradish?"

"I hear that's rough stuff," Annie commented, trying to hide her grin.

"Thank goodness *I* never have any kind of allergic reaction to horseradish," Mr. Mack said. "Wouldn't that be awful? I love horseradish so much, I'd probably eat it anyway."

"Look!" Mrs. Mack pulled up the top piece of bread on his late-night snack. "There's more horseradish on this sandwich than there is cheese!"

Mr. Mack turned around. "Would either of you girls like a horseradish sandwich?" he asked with a chuckle. "Annie? Alex?"

"No, thanks," Alex said honestly. "I never want to eat horseradish again as long as I live!"

The two sisters' shoulders shook with laughter as they ran upstairs to bed.

CHAPTER 14

Alex crawled into bed, thinking of all the things that had happened to her in the past few days.

Alex had called Robyn to apologize, but Robyn was so happy, all she could talk about was the prize she'd won that afternoon for her brownies.

"They gave me a special award—for 'Most Interesting Food Made with an Unusual Ingredient.' Can you believe it? That's exactly what *you* said, Alex, the first time you tried them," Robyn said in amazement. "You said they were 'interesting.' I should know I can always count on you to be straight with me, Alex."

Then she went on to explain that Kelly had been disqualified when one of the judges discovered a cake box from Debbie's Bake Shop on Main Street. And Louis? He got sick from eating too many cookies.

Plus, she added, she'd found out that Chad Kennedy was already going out with two girls from Paradise Valley as well as some girl he met at summer camp who lived in Spartanburg. "What a creep!" Robyn exclaimed. "Alex, you were right to warn me away from him. Thanks for saving me from making a total fool of myself!"

Alex snuggled down into the covers. It was great to see Robyn so happy. *I just hope she doesn't start baking all the time,* Alex thought. *It might really put a strain on our relationship!*

She still had to patch things up with Nicole, but she had a feeling they'd be able to work things out. They'd been friends for a long time—too long to stop speaking over something small.

And she'd still have to be careful for the next few days, till the horseradish-GC-161 combination wore off. *One thing's for sure,* Alex thought, *I'm definitely going to start reading food labels now.* No way was she going to let the tiniest trace of horseradish pass her lips if she could help it.

When Annie got into bed and turned out the light, Alex rolled over onto her stomach and looked out the window at the starry night sky. The once-full moon was now missing a small sliver. She wondered if she would think of honesty—and horseradish!—for the rest of her life whenever she saw a full moon.

"I wonder what it would be like if everyone in the world told the truth all the time," she wondered aloud.

"I don't know," Annie responded. "It would probably be good, once we all got used to it."

Alex thought of the black-and-white cat, wondering if she were already in a new home. "Sometimes I wish we were more like animals. They're just so straight and honest in their dealings with you."

"That's what you think," Annie said.

"What do you mean?"

"For example," Annie explained, "I read once that scientists have studied this bird in South America that has learned to imitate another bird's cry of alarm. So when it sees that the other bird has found food, it imitates the cry of alarm and the other bird flies off—leaving the food for the bird who lied."

"You're kidding!"

"No. Even plants practice deception, if you think about it. Have you ever seen a Venus's-flytrap? It smells like a plant that a fly would want to eat. But when the fly lands on one of the plant's hairy traps, the flytrap snaps it shut so it can devour the fly."

"Ewww!" Alex flopped on her back and pulled the covers up to her chin. "This is too weird to think about!"

"I know, it's bizarre, isn't it?" Annie said. "So maybe lying is just in our nature."

"Maybe, but I guess that's what religion and philosophy are all about. Trying to figure out what we *should* do—not just what's in our nature to do."

"Wow, Alex." Annie giggled. "A profound thought!"

They were silent a moment, each thinking about the last few days.

Then Alex spoke softly into the darkness. "We're

The Secret World of Alex Mack

going to have to tell them the truth about me one of these days, aren't we, Annie?"

"Mom and Dad?"

"Uh-huh."

"Yeah, you're right." Annie sighed. "It's not going to be easy. It's going to upset them. And who knows how our world will change when others know the truth."

"I know. But sometimes I think . . . I'll be glad when Mom and Dad know."

"Yeah, me, too."

"You know what, Annie?" Alex whispered.

"What?"

"I'm glad you're my sister."

Annie was silent for a moment. "Yeah," she said with a catch in her voice. "Me, too."

"And you know what else?"

"What?"

"If you *ever* make me taste another spoonful of horseradish," Alex promised, "I'll break all your test tubes!"

Whomp!

"Alex—!"

The pillow fight that followed was absolutely the best one they'd had since they were little girls.

132

About the Author

Cathy East Dubowski almost always tells the truth—because with her face, people can always tell when she's lying!

Cathy went all out in researching this book and actually baked a batch of Robyn's Wowie Zowie Brownie Surprise—but she recommends that readers *not* try this at home! Like Alex, she and her two daughters, Lauren and Megan, absolutely *hated* them! But her husband, Mark, a cartoonist and children's book illustrator, reacted much like Ray. He ate them with a shrug.

Cathy has written many books for kids, including the Secret World of Alex Mack books *Cleanup Catastrophe!*, *Take a Hike!*, and *Bonjour, Alex!*, and several in the Full House/Michelle series, published by Minstrel Books. One of her original books for younger readers, *Cave Boy*, was named a Children's Book Council/International Reading Association Children's Choice.

Cathy and her family live in North Carolina with their big red golden retriever, Macdougal, and their cocatiel, Birdie.

She is currently at work on a *Sabrina, the Teenage Witch* novel and several other books.

Have you ever wished for the complete guide to surviving your teenage years? At long last, here's your owner's manual—a book of instructions and insights into exactly how YOU operate.

Let's Talk About Me!

A Girl's Personal, Private, and Portable Instruction Book for life

Learn what makes boys so weird
Discover the hidden meanings in your doodles
Uncover the person you want to be
Get to know yourself better than anyone else on Earth
Laugh a little
Think a little
Grow a little

Top-secret quizzes, cool activities, and much, much more

Being a teenage girl
has never been so much fun!

From the creators of
the bestselling CD-ROM!

An Archway Paperback
Published by Pocket Books

1384-01

NICKELODEON

Are You Afraid of the Dark?®

#1 THE TALE OF THE SINISTER STATUES 52545-X/$3.99

#2 THE TALE OF CUTTER'S TREASURE 52729-0/$3.99

#3 THE TALE OF THE RESTLESS HOUSE 52547-6/$3.99

#4 THE TALE OF THE NIGHTLY NEIGHBORS 53445-9/$3.99

#5 THE TALE OF THE SECRET MIRROR 53671-0/$3.99

#6 THE TALE OF THE PHANTOM SCHOOL BUS 53672-9/$3.99

#7 THE TALE OF THE GHOST RIDERS 56252-5/$3.99

#8 THE TALE OF THE DEADLY DIARY 53673-7/$3.99

#9 THE TALE OF THE VIRTUAL NIGHTMARE 00080-2/$3.99

#10 THE TALE OF THE CURIOUS CAT 00081-0/$3.99

#11 THE TALE OF THE ZERO HERO 00357-7/$3.99

#12 THE TALE OF THE SHIMMERING SHELL 00392-5/$3.99

#13 THE TALE OF THE THREE WISHES 00358-5/$3.99

#14 THE TALE OF THE CAMPFIRE VAMPIRES 00908-7/$3.99

#15 THE TALE OF THE BAD-TEMPERED GHOST 01429-3/$3.99

#16 TALE OF THE SOUVENIR SHOP 00909-5/$3.99

A MINSTREL® BOOK

Simon & Schuster Mail Order Dept. BWB
200 Old Tappan Rd., Old Tappan, N.J. 07675

Please send me the books I have checked above. I am enclosing $_____(please add $0.75 to cover the postage and handling for each order. Please add appropriate sales tax). Send check or money order--no cash or C.O.D.'s please. Allow up to six weeks for delivery. For purchase over $10.00 you may use VISA: card number, expiration date and customer signature must be included.

Name _____

Address _____

City _____ State/Zip _____

VISA Card # _____ Exp.Date _____

Signature _____

1053-15

Sometimes, it takes a kid to solve a good crime....

Original stories based on the hit Nickelodeon show!

#1 A Slash in the Night
by Alan Goodman

#2 Takeout Stakeout
By Diana G. Gallagher

#3 Hot Rock
by John Peel

#4 Rock 'n' Roll Robbery
by Lydia C. Marano and David Cody Weiss

To find out more about *The Mystery Files of Shelby Woo* or any other Nickelodeon show, visit Nickelodeon Online on America Online (Keyword: NICK) or send e-mail (NickMailDD@aol.com).

A MINSTREL BOOK

Published by Pocket Books

1338-03